"May I help you?"

"Yes, you may help me. You can tell me what you think you're doing in this houseboat—nude."

One golden-brown eyebrow lifted wickedly, and he answered, "I thought it was obvious. Taking a shower."

"You're not taking one now."

"I'm willing to take another one, if you'll join me."

In an icy voice, Dale told him, "Showering with strangers has never been high on my list of priorities."

"Everyone is a stranger at the first meeting. But we can remedy that in no time at all."

Dale took an involuntary step backward as she battled the insidious web of attraction the man was casting over her . . .

Dear Reader:

By now our new cover treatment—with larger art work—is familiar to you. But don't forget that, in a sense, our new cover reflects what's been happening *inside* SECOND CHANCE AT LOVE books. We're constantly striving to bring you fresh and original romances with unexpected twists and delightful surprises. We introduce promising new writers on a regular basis. And we aim for variety by publishing some romances that are funny, some that are poignant, some that are "traditional," and some that take an entirely new approach. SECOND CHANCE AT LOVE is constantly evolving to meet your need for "something new" in your romance reading.

At the same time, we *haven't* changed the successful editorial concept behind each SECOND CHANCE AT LOVE romance. We work hard to make sure every romance we publish is a satisfying read. And at SECOND CHANCE AT LOVE we've consistently maintained a reputation for being a line of the highest quality.

So, just like the new covers, SECOND CHANCE AT LOVE romances are satisfyingly familiar—yet excitingly different—and better than ever.

Happy reading,

Ellen Edwards

Ellen Edwards, Senior Editor
SECOND CHANCE AT LOVE
The Berkley Publishing Group
200 Madison Avenue
New York, N.Y. 10016

P.S. Do you receive our SECOND CHANCE AT LOVE and TO HAVE AND TO HOLD newsletter? If not, be sure to fill out the coupon in the back of this book, and we'll send you the newsletter free of charge four times a year.

Second Chance at Love

SWEET SPLENDOR

DIANA MARS

SECOND CHANCE AT LOVE
BOOK

Other Second Chance at Love books by
Diana Mars

SWEET SURRENDER #95
SWEET ABANDON #122
SWEET TRESPASS #182

SWEET SPLENDOR

First edition published September 1984

First printing

"Second Chance at Love" and the butterfly emblem are trademarks
belonging to Jove Publications, Inc.

Printed in the United States of America

Second Chance at Love books are published by
The Berkley Publishing Group
200 Madison Avenue, New York, NY 10016

To my grandparents,
Adam and Elisabeth

- 1 -

DALE HAYWARD TURNED on her side, subconsciously ignoring the annoying noise with sleepy irritation. But the noise did not diminish in volume; on the contrary, it increased until not even her defensive maneuver of hiding her head under the pillow could stifle the unmistakable sound of water pelting on tile . . . and of a man singing!

Suddenly, she sat up, the rising off-key baritone cutting through the web of sleep that had cozily enveloped her. She was supposed to be alone in the houseboat!

Indignation left no room for fear or second thoughts as Dale jumped groggily out of bed and marched toward the bathroom without even thinking to put on a robe.

Feeling the rhythmic movement under her bare feet as she traversed the short distance to the bathroom, Dale realized why she had slept so soundly. From the look of the shoreline, the boat had been on the move for quite a while, its soothing, swaying motion perpetuating her sleep. And she'd slept like a baby for the first time in months, blissfully unaware that the *Seaprincess* had been removed from the Sapphire Marina.

The thought of someone encroaching on her private space lit the fuse of her temper. That he'd done it with a raucous volume equaled only by her trusty old alarm clock added fuel to the fire.

As Dale threw open the bathroom door, bouncing it off the ivory wall, the abominable racket ceased abruptly. Her sudden appearance halted the man— who obviously fancied himself Mario Lanza—in the middle of an impossibly convoluted cadenza.

Dale froze in midstep, her mouth gaping. The breath was knocked out of her as her eyes took in the man in the act of shaving before the bathroom mirror, and neither air nor sound issued from her open mouth.

The tableau vivant was broken as the stranger turned from the sink to face her, patting his bronzed cheeks dry. The startled look in his teal-blue eyes was almost immediately replaced by alert curiosity.

With an inward groan, Dale realized that her impetuosity had landed her in another of what her mother used to call her "famous situations." Her failure to knock—indeed, to anticipate anything, especially what was confronting her right now—had resulted in Dale's facing a breathtaking example of virile manhood.

Just how virile was branded into her dazed senses by the fact that the stranger's towel was slung over one muscular shoulder, not wrapped around his narrow hips.

Dale belatedly realized that her fascinated eyes must

have stayed riveted a bit too long in a low line of vision, for the man shattered the silence with a hopeful, suggestive question.

"May I help you?"

To her chagrin, Dale felt a blush warm her softly delineated cheeks. Her gaze flew belatedly to the man's face, vaguely registering in its hurried ascent the sun-browned body, the tapered waist, the broad shoulders, and the strong, corded neck. Crowning this very masculine physique was a rugged face in which a once-broken nose figured prominently in a craggy, surprisingly pleasant countenance.

Her own mint-green eyes widened as she discovered that his gaze was doing a little sight-seeing of its own, but with a lot more leisure and open enjoyment than hers. It seemed a bit silly for her to put up her hands to cover her breasts now. Her jade negligee generously bared them, the sheer ecru lace inset—gathered with elastic and trimmed with bows in twin strategic places—and the high front slit seeming to attract the man's attention like a magnet. Dale noticed with mingled amusement and exasperation that his appreciative eyes were obviously not sure whether to concentrate on her high, full bosom, the long lines of her legs, or the belly button peeping from beneath the plunging V-shaped lace.

As an inner warmth warned her of how surprisingly tempting his offer was, Dale addressed the stranger more sharply than she'd intended.

"Yes, you may help me. You can tell me what you think you're doing in this houseboat—nude."

One golden-brown eyebrow lifted wickedly, and he answered, "I thought it was obvious. Taking a shower."

"You're not taking one now," Dale pointed out, his unruffled composure making tatters of her own.

"I've just finished taking one and was trying to shave." Glancing significantly at the flush that always betrayed Dale when she was embarrassed or excited, then downward past her neck into her luscious cleavage, he added. "But I'm willing to take another one, if you'll join me. Looks like you could do with some cooling down."

Dale regarded him in stunned silence. How could this odious man just stand there, with no shred of clothing on, looking as unconcerned as if he were wearing a three-piece suit? Not that he had anything to be ashamed of, she admitted to herself begrudgingly.

Corralling her galloping thoughts, Dale took a deep breath and straightened her spine, ignoring the interested glance that once more zeroed in on her bustline. In an icy voice she told him, "I'm sure you'll understand if I pass on your offer. Showering with strangers has never been high in my list of priorities."

Taking a step toward her—which somehow managed to increase their intimacy without being threatening—he told her in an inviting, husky voice, "Everyone is a stranger at the first meeting. But we can remedy that in no time at all."

Although not physically afraid, Dale took an involuntary step backward as she battled the insidious web of attraction the man was casting over her. The clean smell of soap and maleness enveloped her with heady potency.

"The only remedy to this is your immediate departure, before I have to add more than trespassing to your offenses," she retorted.

A slight smile crossed the stranger's tanned features as he leaned nonchalantly against the beige sink. Dale stared resentfully at his careless nudity, as against her will she was fascinated by the pattern of golden hair that arrowed lightly down his powerful body.

"There are two things wrong with your alternative," rumbled the rich baritone voice. Dale brought her mind forcibly back to the matter at hand. "First, although we're about the same height, you lack the necessary muscle and gristle to throw me out. Not that I'm complaining, you understand," he added with a widening grin, his glance skimming over her ripe curves once more. "And second, I really don't feel inclined to leave at the moment. I paid for ten days on this boat, where, I might add, I've vacationed for the past four years."

Crossing his arms over his wide chest, he finished softly, "So I guess we're stalemated. And if you don't like the prospect of us getting better acquainted, I guess *you'll* have to leave."

Storms gathered in Dale's eyes, but the man seemed impervious to her visual darts, his teeth flashing white against his bronzed skin. Seeing her dreams of a solitary vacation go up in smoke, she told him with quiet determination, "I am *not* leaving. I'm entitled to a week on this boat, and that's what I'm getting."

"Not alone, you're not," he countered.

Dale's fists knotted at her sides. She found she was having great trouble keeping her volatile temper in check in the face of his rocklike obstinacy. About to repeat that he had no right on the boat, Dale abruptly desisted. The bathroom was really not the place to try to reason with this man—if, indeed, he could be reasoned with. Perhaps if they were both conventionally covered up and in a more appropriate setting, the situation could be defused.

"I'm glad you've realized you're in no position to demand anything," he told her with infuriating confidence.

As the fingers she'd forced to relax began to curl again in anger, it dawned on Dale that he was enjoying nettling her. Usually, it was the other way around. Men tended to pacify her rather than provoke her, apparently intimidated by her height, intelligence, and assertiveness. The blond stranger was markedly different.

And although at the moment her dearest wish was to throttle him, Dale sensed a trustworthy quality about the man that went beyond his rakish, "body beautiful" appearance. Maybe there was some hope after all.

She pivoted, intending to leave with as much dignity as she could muster, given that the man was still stark naked and she revealingly gowned. Outside the door, she turned and told him, "We need to discuss this impasse in other surroundings. I suggest you get decent."

A deep chuckle erupted from his throat, and with a devilish glint in his darkened gaze, the man told her, "I've barely avoided embarrassing you, beautiful. Decency is an impossibility."

Tearing her eyes from the portion of his anatomy that gave credence to his frank statement, Dale fairly fled to her bedroom. His rich, gritty laughter resonated in her ears as she slammed the door shut. Not that she was afraid the man would follow her, but the solid sound of wood on wood was eminently satisfying.

Dale took a few minutes to recover her poise, sinking down on the bed she had so recently and blissfully occupied. She relived the past few minutes' conversation, and a smile began to curve her full pink lips as she acknowledged to herself that it had been pretty absurd.

Not only had she actually stood in a tiny bathroom and told a naked stranger to get out, but that same stranger had made a pass at her—and she hadn't been afraid. At first, his potential threat had been superseded by the other sensations evoked when she'd thrown open the door. Later, he'd aroused such pure, unadulterated fury in her that she'd had to draw on the reserves that had seen her through in her unpredictable job as meeting planner. Not even underbooking or lost audio-visual equipment had brought forth such a torrent of emotion.

But then, Dale recognized, no conventioneer had ever looked like the stranger—nor had she been propositioned in the middle of solving or preventing a crisis.

After rolling her shoulders back and forth and pivoting her head first clockwise, then counterclockwise, to loosen the tension she ruefully identified as being partly sexual, Dale got up slowly and walked to her suitcase, extracting a thick robe.

As she'd brought only casual clothes, she hadn't bothered to unpack the previous evening. Falling instantly in love with her floating home upon boarding it, Dale had explored the *Seaprincess* at leisure, familiarizing herself with the setup. After watching the sunset from her vantage point in the back porch, she had decided on an early night. Wyatt Martin, the Sapphire Marina proprietor, was to have given her pilotage instructions before she set out in the morning, and she had so looked forward to her private adventure that she had even forgone her usual bedtime reading.

Slipping on her green chenille robe, Dale promised herself that she wouldn't let the stranger ruin her vacation. She hadn't had one in over two years and she needed the time away, not only to rest, but also to make a very important decision about her job. She'd been offered a promotion, and although she looked forward to the higher salary and added responsibilities, the new position would entail moving to another state. And she'd just finished furnishing the town house she'd purchased seven months ago.

As she walked to the door, Dale noticed they were no longer stationary—the man had probably anchored the *Seaprincess* while taking his shower—but were moving slowly forward. Her hand remained for a few seconds on the doorknob, and Dale was surprised at its slight tremble. Used to dealing with men, she was not easily dismayed. But she knew it wasn't so much fear of the man that made her nervous as worry over her own reaction to him.

How should a twenty-eight-year-old woman, on her own since she was eighteen and successfully climbing the business ladder, deal with an unaccustomed and frighteningly intense desire for a perfect stranger? And furthermore, how did a supposedly sophisticated woman keep her eyes from masculine flesh that had been visibly susceptible to her own attractions? Especially, she told herself wryly, when that same male made no effort to hide his reaction nor to apologize for it?

As her suddenly sweaty palm slipped on the doorknob, Dale squared her shoulders. She had not achieved the successes of the past ten years by living on the periphery of life. She had always plunged in. Full steam ahead.

Determinedly, Dale opened the door and followed the welcome aroma of brewing coffee to its source. A cup of coffee will restore my equilibrium, she told herself bracingly. All I have to remember is that this man is a stranger and that I really, truly, want him off this boat. Personal and physical magnetism notwithstanding . . .

"That's impossible."

As she spoke, Dale set the half-full cup—her third in half an hour—on the tortoiseshell Formica table with a loud bang.

They were sitting in the spacious galley, he keeping an eye on the boat he'd put on automatic pilot, she by now hugging the edge of the brown settee. Her eyes searched the yellow and brown kitchen, with its double stainless-steel sink and four-burner LP stove featuring an overhead oven and built-in rotisserie, for inspiration and patience.

She found neither.

"Have you even paid the slightest attention to what I've been saying?" she asked in a low voice. Her head was spinning from the circumnavigation the self-satisfied creature had forced on her. He'd had her going in circles since he'd introduced himself as Burke Sheridan only thirty minutes ago, and at this point in the stalemated situation, Dale was finding the effort to remain reasonable highly taxing.

Burke Sheridan nodded calmly. "Sure I have. Wyatt Martin rented the houseboat to you. You wanted to get away for a few days, were able to do so at the last minute and were lucky to get a cancelation—but unlucky at being assigned this particular boat, which Wyatt always reserves for me." In a softened tone, he continued, "And I understand that it's not only your desire to cruise the Mississippi that got you away from Iowa, but also the need for some time by yourself."

Dale took her eyes away from the teak cabinets she'd been studying while listening with contained impatience and leaned forward eagerly. She was pleased to see that her position was finally penetrating that conveniently dense skull.

"However," he said, forestalling her, his grin working on her nerves like sandpaper, "that still leaves me out in the cold. I also expected to be able to count on ten days out of the rat race. I fly in to Iowa at this time every summer, and Wyatt, old friend that he is, knows to expect me. I'm not about to break tradition just because Wyatt's assistant got our dates confused and overlapped our bookings."

Having delivered his ultimatum, Burke settled back complacently. Dale watched with narrowed eyes as he managed to sprawl on the straight-backed chair. At least he'd put on a robe, but its careless tying left her in no doubt that he had nothing else on underneath.

She knew he was a man of contrasts. His well-built body and casual blond hair reminded her of a beachboy, minus the bulging muscles. But inside the cat-lazy body lay quickness and strength, and behind the beautiful aquamarine eyes resided an intelligence and astuteness Dale knew she'd better not treat lightly.

She decided to appeal to his elusive sense of decency. With a soft entreaty in her voice, she said, "Won't you reconsider your decision, Mr. Sher—

Burke? You know I rushed all this past week, worked ungodly hours to be able to leave early on Friday and spend the night here instead of in my town house."

At his raised eyebrows, she said defensively, "Wyatt said renters are welcome to come in between eight and ten the evening prior to the cruise, to spend a relaxing night—"

"I just bet he did."

"—aboard the houseboat," Dale finished, trying to hold on to the softness in her voice. "As you can imagine, it was quite a surprise for me to wake up this morning with a stranger on board. Here I was thinking I'd be given a shakedown cruise with operating instructions before departing, and the boat was already under way."

"Oh, I can understand your feelings, all right," Burke said agreeably. "When I came in late last night, all I wanted to do was get this boat away from civilization fast. I didn't even bother to unpack or check the bedrooms."

This was not going according to plan. He was obviously immune to the soft sell, and Dale had to admit ruefully that the soft sell had never been her forte in any case.

Asperity climbing into her tone astride frustration, she told him, "We've been through this before."

"But you were just seeing if sugar would work where vinegar hadn't?"

"If you consider me such a bitter potion, why don't you just leave? Unlike you, I'd be quite glad to turn around and take you back to the marina, where you could make alternate plans." *Or go to hell,* she added silently.

"Ahh, now we're getting there," Burke told her

amiably, a dimple carving his chiseled cheekbone. Dale glared at it. Sexy voice, gorgeous body, antique-gold hair—and a dimple, too.

"From what I can see, we're getting nowhere fast," she remarked tartly.

"On the contrary," Burke disagreed, leaning forward, his body suffocatingly close as he picked up his cup. Her fascinated gaze observed the cords of his neck standing out under the brown skin as he gulped down a healthy swallow of coffee. "You've just confirmed my first impression. I took you for a straight shooter. Seems I was right. You sure dropped your ingratiating act soon enough."

"Which proves nothing except that I'm not a good social liar." Interlacing her fingers in her lap, Dale rubbed them against the soft chenille of her robe and added accusingly, "But it doesn't get us any closer to a solution—unless you agree to go back."

"What about *you* going back?"

"You know that at this late date I wouldn't be able to rent another..." Her impatient words died at the look on his face. *Great going, Dale!*

His laughing eyes checked the river quickly before alighting on her once more.

"How *did* you manage to snag the *Seaprincess* at the last minute?"

"A couple was supposed to take it for their honeymoon, but had to cancel when the groom came down with chicken pox."

A rich, throaty gust of laughter erupted fullblown from Burke, and Dale found herself smiling in response. "That's not funny," she chided. "I had it when I was sixteen and it was no picnic. Not only was the itching worse and more prolonged, but the older one gets, the more dangerous it is to come down with a contagious disease."

"I'm sure the poor groom was bemoaning more than one itch," Burke told her wickedly.

"What about the bride...?" Dale began, before his meaning registered. "You're awful."

Her severity had no effect on him. Burke had a renewed laughing bout, and Dale found it hard not to join in. She found the sound of his deep chuckles playing like fresh, bubbly champagne on her skin. As she studied him silently she was unwillingly attracted to his joie de vivre. Such spontaneous mirth seemed lost to a lot of businessmen she knew—or else it was artificially induced by alcohol.

Unthinkingly, she asked him, "Do you drink?"

Burke looked at her blankly for a moment, his eyes still retaining the amusement that carved deep laugh lines along them. "Drink? As in gin, Scotch?"

Dale nodded, her gaze purposely evading the broad chest exposed to her view. The bronzed skin and golden hair contrasted enticingly with the maroon material of his robe.

"No, I don't," he answered seriously, getting up for a moment to take a close look out the window. Dale followed his gaze and saw a small pleasure craft, the first she'd spotted since joining Burke in the kitchen, but it quickly pulled into an inlet and disappeared from view. Resuming his position, Burke told her, "And even though I'm partial to Junoesque brunettes with tropical-green eyes, you don't have to worry about being assaulted. I've never forced a woman and don't intend to start now. If we share the houseboat, you'll be as safe as in your home. You have my promise that if we become involved, it will only be at your instigation."

Dale inhaled sharply. The thought that he'd attack her had not been on her mind; she hadn't needed his assurance on that. But his certainty of a possible involvement stung, particularly since it was grounded in reality. Day in and day out proximity with a man like Burke precluded sane thinking. And thinking was what she'd hoped to accomplish in the next few days.

She knew Burke was waiting for her decision, but Dale could see no easy solution. Gazing sightlessly at the wide expanse of water that beat unceasingly at verdant slopes and flung itself back to lap and gurgle against the boat, she sighed. Her hand impatiently going to the black hair she'd tied at the nape with a silk scarf and that continuously invaded the collar of her neck, Dale raised her eyes and saw that Burke was staring at her with unsettling intensity. Her skin began to feel prickly under his steady regard, and she quickly freed the silky strands that rubbed against her sensitive skin each time she moved.

"I was not concerned about my safety," she finally said, her eyes meeting Burke's levelly. "I know you've had plenty of chances. What does concern me is the occupancy of this houseboat—and the fact that we might become involved."

"You don't want to become involved?" Burke questioned softly.

An image of Joel sprang unbidden to her mind. With a jolt, she realized that Burke reminded her of the carefree lover who'd taken all she'd had to give— until there had been no more.

"No," she said flatly. "And I'm neither young nor

foolish enough to believe that forced intimacy might not have some repercussions."

"Why not go with the tide, then?" he asked. "Unless you have some prior commitment on land."

No, she had no prior commitment. And she liked keeping it that way. Ignoring his probing into her personal life, she asked instead, "Are you sure you have to leave the country immediately at the end of your vacation?"

Burke held her gaze. "I was lucky even to be granted the brief vacation between my two assignments. Only by threatening to quit was I able to get these few days before I return to Saudi Arabia."

Dale found the latent power of the large, tanned body resting with deceptive looseness across the table more disquieting than any amount of movement could have been. Whereas she had to discipline herself to remain still, conservation of energy seemed to be a part of Burke's makeup.

"Then I guess there's no other way. You'll have to let me off at the next port," Dale told him in a resigned tone, even as her mind raced furiously. Although Burke was holding all the cards now—namely, his greater physical strength—he had to have an Achilles' heel. All she had to do was find it and neutralize it. After all, wasn't that what she was good at—problem solving?

His warm hand on her arm jolted her out of her contemplation. "Listen," Burke said quickly. At her pointed look, he slowly removed his hand but remained close to her. "Why not give it a chance for a day or two? After all, this boat is designed for four people. We should be able to keep out of each other's way for twenty-four hours. That way, you'll at least get a taste of houseboating before you go back. And maybe you'll even find we're sufficiently compatible that you'll decide to spend the rest of your vacation on the *Seaprincess*."

"Why would you want me on board?" Dale asked suspiciously. "You told me you had also counted on solitude, and some quiet fishing and exploring."

His smile was wolfish. "There are several reasons, the most obvious being that I'd be able to stare back at you every day—raven hair, light eyes, almost six feet of breathtaking curves..."

"What I look like has no bearing on this discussion," she inserted primly, then amended with reluctant amusement at the light in his eyes, "or at least it shouldn't. Besides, I suspect you like the coloring of the one you're with, as the song goes."

"Mea culpa," he intoned irresistibly. His large hand dwarfed the crystal mug as he swallowed the last of the coffee and took another quick look outside. "But really, I do feel bad about curtailing your vacation. We are, so to speak, in the same boat."

He grinned as she winced at his pun, and leaned forward. "Will you please reconsider?"

Dale's gaze locked with Burke's. The appeal in his blue-green eyes was hard to ignore. To escape it, Dale turned to look at the lonely, empty stretch of river and the surrounding emerald banks. Either way, she reflected, whether she stayed or left, she lost. Yet, she didn't want to contemplate foregoing her houseboating vacation, since at this late date, it meant no vacation at all. What a choice!

Unless...

Her eyes flashed green fire before she concealed them behind a profuse veil of dark lashes. Adopting a neutral expression, she said, "All right."

"All right?"

The cautious echo told Dale she'd been right in not underestimating Burke Sheridan. She would have to work hard to lull him to complacency.

"We'll try it your way and see what happens."

"Thank you—I *think*," Burke said slowly. Getting up and gathering the cups and coffeepot, he told her, "I'll try to stay out of your way and not inconvenience you in any manner."

Rising stiffly, Dale refrained from telling him she was already inconvenienced. Burke certainly appeared sincere enough. And although, from what he'd said, he had not always been unaccompanied on previous trips, he did seem a bit exhausted. She supposed even a man like Burke had to rest up from the chase— recharge his batteries, as it were.

But, she promised herself as she retied the sash of her robe around her slender waist in eloquent vehemence, Burke was going to find one female who did not flip over his golden presence. Most women dreamed of men like Burke—adventurers, irresistibly male— but she'd had her quota in Joel. Men like her ex-fiancé and Burke Sheridan might be exciting, but after the excitement palled, nothing was left. At least for the woman. She'd gone through three years of living life in an emotional fast lane. And when she'd finally left Joel two years ago, she'd known the meaning of the word *heartbreaker*.

But the trouble was, heartbreakers only broke other people's hearts. Theirs were inviolable.

As Burke turned from the sink where he'd deposited the dishes, she realized belatedly that he'd said something. Her eyes met gleaming blue-green ones which first caressed her bemused features, then journeyed slowly downward to her throat, where a pulse beat betrayingly.

Dale had to fight waves of sensual lassitude to extricate herself, but this time she didn't resent the surge of color radiating outward from her inner heat. She used it to her advantage, letting Burke think she was on her way to becoming infatuated. That should put him off guard, even if he did have an inkling of something.

She saw his firm lips move, and caught the tail end of his words.

". . . how do you like your eggs?"

The mundane question disconcerted her. She asked, "Eggs?" Then, when the import of the words penetrated her mind, she inquired skeptically, "You can cook?"

"I'm a great cook. Will that make it easier for you to accept me as an impromptu roommate?"

"Boatmate," Dale corrected wryly. "And you know what they say: 'The way to a woman's heart . . .'"

"I'll keep that in mind," Burke promised softly.

- 2 -

DALE STUDIED BURKE silently as he guided the boat with easy expertise down the Illinois Waterway. Their journey south was certainly a smooth one under his pilotage. The sun glinted off the olive-green river and cast on his browned flesh shadows that undulated over a wiry network of muscles, which were seductively sprinkled with fair masculine hair.

Breakfast had been a pleasant, indolent affair in which Burke had demonstrated that he was not only a terrific cook but also a witty conversationalist. And having discovered that conversation seemed a lost art on the dates she'd had since her breakup with Joel, Dale found their exchange too dangerously enjoyable. But not too personally illuminating. Burke seemed to be a private person, as she herself was.

With a start, Dale realized she'd given very little thought to the decision she'd hoped to arrive at during her vacation. Her promotion entailed a move to St.

Louis, and although she'd been in St. Louis before and it certainly was not an earthshaking move, such as going to New York or Los Angeles would have represented, there were several factors to consider.

Her family and friends were in Iowa; still, she'd always been independent, going to an out-of-state university to nurture that independence. But it had taken her time to rebuild her life in the past two years, and work had assumed a major importance in her life. She liked her job, combining as it did travel and variety. As a meeting planner, she got to stay at major hotels and resorts in Iowa and sometimes in neighboring states. But she always came back to home base—in the past few months, a town house that reflected her taste and personality.

She liked her life—and her job—as it was. And now Harvey Nesmond, who'd had the opportunity to see her meeting-planner abilities at a top-level executive convention she'd handled the year before, was threatening to throw her life into turmoil again and doing so with an offer so attractive she couldn't just quickly and summarily dismiss it . . .

"Thinking about setting down your memoirs?"

The light baritone voice brought Dale out of her reverie, and she raised pensive eyes from the white knit shirt hugging Burke's well-defined chest.

"Maybe. And you'd certainly play a part in it. I've never had a more delicious breakfast."

"Liked my hash browns, did you?" Burke asked, grinning. "In exchange, I expect to try a specialty of yours."

"Then you're bound to be disappointed." Dale laughed, thinking of her limited cooking repertoire. "The only thing that can be considered my specialty—

meaning I manage not to burn it or undercook it—is a barbecued steak or hot dog over an open fire."

Burke returned his eyes to the river and said thoughtfully, "That can be arranged. We can put in at some deserted spot and I can build a campfire."

"Oh, I know how to do that," Dale said, her mind working feverishly. "Just find us a suitable spot."

"Aye, aye, Captain," Burke replied, a faint smile curving his hard, sensuous lips, his glittering gaze leaving the river for a brief instant.

In those few seconds, his glance thoroughly skated over her form, taking in her brief white shorts and orange-flame halter, and she discovered to her dismay that she was minding his appreciative scrutiny less and less. Which didn't bode well for the execution of her plan.

She stepped forward, moving to his right as he skillfully maneuvered his way past a small central island. Gazing wistfully backward at the alluring cluster of verdant islands they were leaving behind and that she'd be exploring right now had she been alone, she murmured, "It's beautiful, isn't it? So peaceful, one can almost feel jagged nerves being brought to life again."

Some of her longing must have shown in her voice, because Burke gave her a quick, searching glance. "If there's anything that interests you, please don't hesitate to ask me to stop. I plan to take in some fishing, which will undoubtedly prove boring or confining to you. And there's enough scenic treasure—especially on Old Man River—to keep us both happy."

Dale didn't answer at first. She'd never fancied fishing, and knowing that Burke expected her to put in at any cove that looked properly fertile in aquatic

life did a lot to renew her sense of purpose. Relaxing
next to him, letting his virile magnetism bathe her
with the same warmth the sun was dispensing, was
proving to be a sensual sedative. And she needed her
sagacity unimpaired if she expected to catch Burke
off *his* guard.

When she didn't answer, Burke fixed her with a
penetrating gaze and asked, "Agreed?"

"Agreed," she replied blandly to stave off suspicion. He took his right hand from the wheel and thrust
it in front of her. Dale hesitated, but when Burke's
eyes dropped to his extended hand and lifted again to
her, brows arching questioningly, she placed her hand
in his. Hoping her inner reluctance didn't show, she
essayed a strong, quick pump but found that the large,
masculine hand, which engulfed hers completely, did
not constrain itself to a businesslike squeeze. It lin-
gered, the rough calluses of his palm and the circling
motion of his thumb on the tender flesh of her wrist
initiating an erotic tingle that spread upward.

"On one condition," she added hastily, when a
second tug on her hand produced similar results.

Burke let go of her hand, and as he deftly turned
the boat at a bend of the river asked, "And that is . . . ?"

"That you refrain from your impulses, or perhaps
a better term may be *habits*, like the one just now. I
can't stop you from looking, I suppose, but I draw
the line at seduction."

Casting a glance at her that encompassed Dale's
long legs, her knees tucked under her chin, her arms
holding them within the tiny confines of her seat, he
asked softly. "In other words, look but don't touch?
Lady, you've made my blood boil since the minute I

first laid eyes on you—and believe me, I'd have loved to have laid more than eyes on you."

Dale surveyed him as he negotiated another sharp bend. The river, previously fairly regular, now seemed to reflect her own tortuous thoughts and emotions. Burke's husky tone, potent masculinity, and frank, provocative words all combined to initiate a diffuse longing that seared her loins and put her on edge sexually.

But she'd been through something like this before. And she'd sworn not to make the same mistake again.

Pushing down on the hot urges and the inexplicable twinges of guilt that assailed her, she told him with false brightness, "Your libido will survive."

His tone was wry. "You expect me to pilot with blinders on?"

"Why not?" she returned lightly. "Just go over some of the more salient points of navigation with me, and you can leave the driving to me."

"You mean you were going off without the proper training? Wyatt—or any other houseboat renter— would never allow you out of the marina without instruction, let alone on a seven-day jaunt. Even if you were experienced in riverboating, which you aren't. Each section of river is different and—"

"Wyatt didn't *allow* me. I got a brief orientation from him when I drove by the marina a couple of weeks ago to see if it was still possible to rent for July. He was reviewing the workings of a boat with a couple who'd gone houseboating the year before." Her voice was sternly accusing as she told him, "He was to go into more detailed instruction, as well as to suggest promising side trips and enumerate the boundaries within which the boat must be operated under the charter and insurance agreements. *This* morning."

"Which just goes to show that you can't leave things till the last minute," Burke said, his grin slashing deep parallel lines in his lean, tanned cheeks.

"Burke Sheridan," Dale grated, eyeing his powerful back sourly, "if you knew the hours I had to put in to get away in July, the height of the convention season in many cities—"

Burke put up his hand in a gesture of peace and said laughingly, "All right. All right. I'm sorry. Next time I come aboard late at night, I'll check both bedrooms to see if the gods have been generous again and presented me with as delicious a roommate as they did this time."

While Dale stared at him openmouthed, he turned and gave her a quick wink and a slow grin. "Think of the time we've wasted. I have the feeling you're more approachable with a kiss in the mornings. And instead I had to put you out of sorts with my off-key singing, an unfortunate inheritance from my mother."

Dale closed her mouth, narrowed her eyes, and licked her lips. She was not sure which issue to take up first.

"Ahhh." He turned back to the river. "So nice to see you speechless for once. That tongue of yours looks luscious when you lick your lips"—Dale swiftly drew her offending appendage back into her mouth— "but it can sure deliver stinging repartee."

"Never mind my tongue—or other portions of my anatomy," Dale retorted. "I thought you promised to behave."

"I'm keeping my hands on the wheel."

"Too bad you can't keep your mind on the right track, too."

"But I am on the right track. I've got you beside me, haven't I?"

Dale shook her head and stood up, liking the slight sway of the deck under her feet. "How about filling me in on the parts I missed from my orientation?"

Sighing, Burke relinquished the wheel with dramatized reluctance. "I'm not sure about this. As long as I carry all the knowledge around here, I'm needed. I've always thought a little knowledge in a woman's hands is a dangerous thing."

Dale glanced sharply at him, but his eyes appeared guileless. Her pulse quickened as she wondered whether his remark had been an idle comment or whether he did actually suspect something.

But he didn't allow her to dwell on that line of thought as he began to explain the functioning of the craft, its basic layout, and the various dangers to be encountered on the Mississippi and its tributaries.

Over the next half-hour, Burke interspersed the dull, boring facts of the boat's layout and maintenance with stories illustrating the hazards likely to be encountered. Some had happened to him, some to friends, but Burke infused all the anecdotes with the ready sense of humor that was such an integral part of his forceful personality.

As Burke told her about keeping a weather eye for rocks, sunken logs, and reefs; to learn to scan ahead for indications of what lay beneath, especially in shallow waters; to be on the constant lookout for hazards too recent or transient to have been mapped or buoyed, Dale found herself listening intently to his precise instructions with one part of her, while another, truant part registered nuances of sound, inflection, and expression on his arresting face.

When she found her attention wandering as he spoke of tides and currents, seasonal changes, and wind direction, she recalled herself to time and place abruptly, reminding herself once more that she'd be in need of this information later. To convince both Burke and herself that she thoroughly understood what he had been telling her, she asked, "Do we have a depth finder on board?"

"Yep. But you still have to be careful when the boat draws close to the charted depths. You should watch the boat's wake, too. When entering shallow water, a wake becomes jaggedly peaked and its pattern turns irregular."

"Have you ever had to seek local information?" she asked, inhaling deeply of the river fragrance, which combined with Burke's own musky scent to create a heady aroma.

"A couple of times, once in Florida, the second about three years back. That's why I keep a two-way radio on board."

Taking her eyes from the smoothly flowing waters for an instant, she glanced at his relaxed face. His smile of reminiscence brought into play the male lines about his eyes and mouth. "What happened?"

"A river is constantly in a state of flux, and when it erodes, it holds in suspension masses of sediment that it unloads when it meets some obstacle. I ran aground on one of the shoals that continuously form along banks and inside bends."

Dale watched him as he gazed at the sky again, observing that he'd done it several times since he'd begun his expert instruction.

"Were you able to get out?" she asked him.

"It took a couple of hours of pushing and shoving, but I was able to get off the sandbank, and luckily both the propeller and hull were okay."

His hands closing about her wrists lightly, he added almost as an afterthought, "It's dangerous sometimes for a woman alone to go into unfrequented tributaries or too close to islands. If you get grounded, you may need more than the engine to get you going again. You may have to push the boat off the obstruction or shift weight to the back of the boat farthest from the problem spot and toss or row the anchor out into deep water, trying to work the boat free by pulling on the anchor line. It requires muscle power, and it could be some time before the help you requested over the radio phone arrives, if no passing boat is nearby to provide a tow."

Dale digested this information silently, telling herself she was reading too much into its general warnings. Still, she thought it politic to change the subject. She removed Burke's hands, which were ostensibly teaching her how to guide the wheel but which had by now climbed slowly to her elbows and had nestled against the soft inner skin.

"I don't drive with my elbows, Burke," she told him wryly. He dropped his hands from her arms and moved away from her—only to stand to her side so that he could study her at his leisure. His hot glance was discomposing, but Dale knew that, short of shoving him into the river, she had no recourse but to grin and bear it. Grin she did, with what she feared was a ludicrous parody of a smile.

"Why the constant lookout on the sky?" She asked him. "I noticed you've been watching it like a hawk, all but sniffing the air. How come? It looks beautiful today, and sunny weather was predicted for the rest of the week."

Burke put his arm about her waist, the hairs on his arms producing an intense tickle on the velvety flesh exposed by the halter. "The air's getting heavier. We may have a cloudless sky, but it's going to rain. If not tomorrow, then the next day."

Puzzled, Dale watched as he removed her gently from the wheel and steered the boat to the side of the river. She ducked from under his encircling arms, but Burke brushed her cheek with a quick forefinger before she moved away.

"Haven't you heard the latest on human cravings?" he asked as he dropped anchor, anticipating the ready words on her lips. "Studies are being done at respected institutions of higher learning that categorically prove that human beings need to be hugged more."

Dale stood looking at him with arms crossed over her chest, waiting for him to explain his halting in this rather desolate section of shore. Her skeptical eyes conveyed clearly what she thought of this new gambit.

He returned to her side. "You know, monkeys can die without touch, and babies can't develop properly without the right amount of affection and stimulation..."

Dale stood her ground. "You and I are not babies and you don't seem to have suffered from any deprivation or lack of stimulation," she told him. "If anything, your cravings might have been satisfied too easily."

Burke chuckled, smoothing a stubborn lock of hair back from her damp forehead.

"But I starve for affection when I'm on assignment

in godforsaken parts of the world," he said, grinning. "Men aren't too keen on other men asking them if they want to be hugged."

"I can imagine not."

"See, you do understand," he put in, his errant hand leaving her hair and beginning to trace delicate patterns on her forehead and upturned nose. Dale shook her head as if disposing of a nettlesome fly, but the practiced fingers continued their implacable descent down her cheeks and finally to her lips, marking their moist fullness. His forefinger eased into her parted mouth, butterfly-soft, stroking the pearly smoothness of her teeth before caressing the tip of her tongue.

Dale swallowed convulsively and stepped away from him, hoping the tremor that rippled through her frame had been disguised by her hasty movement.

Burke's blue-green eyes, glinting with amusement and male knowledge, told her it hadn't.

The small silence that followed was heavy and humid with sexual tension, and the fine beads of perspiration that glistened on her upper lip and the valley between her breasts owed little to the heat of the sun.

Burke leaned against the door to the galley and said, his eyes never leaving hers, "I figured you wouldn't mind if we stopped for a few hours. This is a great place for fishing. It might not be the most picturesque spot on the entire route, but the next stop will be one of your choice."

Dale tore her gaze from him and inspected the bland, insipid stretch of land Burke had parked them in. Of all the possible places to stop—sections with lush vegetation and a myriad wild flowers, or craggy bluffs that invited exploration, or small waterfalls that enticed the traveler to try their cool cascades—Burke seemed to have picked the least attractive.

But not knowing anything about fishing, except that she thought it an awful waste when it was only pursued for trophies, she was not going to demur. Besides, this could prove to be her chance.

Nodding silently, she moved to walk past him. But Burke's arm snaked out, effectively preventing her passage.

"Where are you going?"

His question, devoid of his usual light mockery or wry amusement, surprised her, and she paused scant inches from him.

"To change. If you want to fish, go right ahead. I'd rather sunbathe and read for a while."

"Excellent idea," he said approvingly. "Go ahead and change into your bikini. My fishing lessons can wait."

"Lust before sport?" she couldn't resist asking. "And how would you know I own a bikini?"

"Oh, come now. A figure as delectable as yours is made to display—and from the rest of the wardrobe I've been privileged to view so far, I'd say you're not loath to show it off."

His being right didn't endear him to her. She *was* proud of her figure, and enjoyed silky, flowing, sometimes revealing clothes that emphasized the fact. At least, outside of work. But there was no need for him to hammer the point home.

Telling herself that silence was golden in this instance, Dale stood stoically, her eyes digging into the bronzed muscular limb that barred her way. When it didn't disappear under her visual bombardment, she raised the full artillery of her green gaze and submitted him to its lethal force.

"Ouch," he exclaimed, slowly lowering his arm. "What those eyes would do in the heat of passion."

Her eyes changing to green ice, she said coolly as she swept regally past him. "Something you're unlikely to find out."

She didn't stop at his first statement, uttered with complacent amusement—"A man can dream, can't he?"—but did halt her military march down the hall at his next one.

"Oh, by the way, I got in touch with Wyatt while you were getting . . . decent this morning." With hateful suggestiveness, he repeated the phrase she had used earlier. "I knew he'd worry when you didn't show up for orientation this morning. I let him know we're sharing the boat and that you've been a real sport about this." Dale's back, still turned to him, underwent an instant realignment at his gall. "Wyatt was none too happy at my taking up the tutelage, and told me to pass on a message to you . . . to be careful with me."

She turned at this, her eyebrows arching at his words. "He also said he was sorry for the mix-up and won't charge you anything for the trip."

As her eyes widened at this news Burke added with a wicked grin, "You're really lethal, beautiful. Those smoldering green eyes work fast."

"I'm sure I don't know—and don't care to know—what you mean by that."

Burke told her anyway as she turned to leave. "Simple. Wyatt was livid when I told him I'd be teaching you the more advanced maneuvers. I guess he was looking forward to doing it himself."

Her head turned so sharply at this that her neck hurt. "Aren't you assuming too much, *Mister* Sheridan? A woman doesn't get to be twenty-eight without knowing some of the moves." She thought of Wyatt Martin—late thirties, handsome, charming—and flushed angrily as she imagined what he must be thinking.

"I don't doubt it. You're obviously able to handle men and must do so every day in your job." The look she threw him said, There you have it. "But there are always new moves to be learned. And I'm told I make as excellent a student as I am a teacher."

Dale looked at him for a long moment, resolve hardening within her. Oh, that damn charm! The sensual smile on the well-formed lips and the playful sexual challenge in the teal-blue eyes were reminiscent of another arresting face—only that one had had black eyes and curly ebony hair. Joel's.

"Well, scratch modesty as another of the virtues you possess," she said, pushing away the unwelcome flash of memory. "I just wonder, if this is your example of behaving, what you're like when you make a *heavy* pass."

Taking a step toward her, he asked softly, "Shall I show you?"

Dale put out a hand to ward him off. "Thank you, no, I'll deprive myself. Go catch some fish."

As she started toward her bedroom, his words drifted to her.

"I'd rather catch a mammal. They're warm-blooded—if not necessarily warmhearted."

- 3 -

DALE TOOK OFF her shorts and halter with jerky movements filled with fury and resolution. As she shoved on the two minute scraps of black netting, she began to form a plan in her mind.

She was fairly confident of being able to handle the *Seaprincess* after listening to Burke's clear directions. But she was not so sure about Burke. Several times during his tutoring, she'd had the feeling he was weighing her, studying her. And some of his comments had taken on the nature of warnings in her guilt-ridden mind.

Pulling her thick mane of hair over one shoulder, Dale began braiding it, letting the familiar task soothe her. She walked over to the suitcase that still lay on the twin bunk and that she still hadn't unpacked, and absently extracted a length of ribbon. As she went to stand in front of the mirror above the dresser to tie her hair in a ponytail, she noticed that the ribbon was

33

green, a shade darker than her eyes. Quickly tying a secure knot, she picked up her sunglasses, glad they were of the mirror-lensed variety so that she could hide her scheming from Burke. Then, selecting two paperback novels from the stack on the small dresser, she walked to the door.

Just as she opened the door, she remembered she hadn't taken her tanning lotion with her and went back inside. She retraced her steps, smiling, recalling the time in Mexico when she'd turned shrimp red, matching the *camarones* Joel had insisted she try. She paused for a surprised moment, her hand on the doorknob, her mind adjusting to the fact that she'd been able to remember the incident without bitterness. Time had done its healing. But it had not erased the lesson she'd learned when Joel had postponed the wedding for the third and final time. And she'd do well to remember the similarities between Joel and Burke, she told herself firmly as she stepped out the door—and smacked right into a hard, warmly breathing wall.

Burke put out his hands instinctively to catch her as she bounced right off him, and her books, sunglasses, and lotion jumped from her grasp and landed with deadly accuracy on his bare toes.

He managed to strangle a colorful curse in midcourse and change it to a relatively milder "dammit all to hell," but Dale had heard enough of his vivid expletive to guess at the rest. His valiant attempt at gentlemanly conduct, plus the way he hopped from foot to foot under the barrage of missiles, momentarily erased all designing and resolutions from her mind, and she burst into genuine, unrestrained laughter.

Without her sandals she was an inch or so shorter than Burke, and she gazed up at him, her body still shaking from her mirth, to find him frowning down at her. His obvious displeasure only increased her enjoyment, but her lightheartedness was curtailed when she saw the pain and irritation disappear from his face, replaced by dawning physical awareness.

Dale noticed belatedly that he must have been tugging on his T-shirt, because the blue material was hunched up under his arms. Her palms were lying flat against his chest, her fingers splayed on the crinkly golden cloud of fine hair. The breath that had been squeezed out of her in their collision and in her laughing bout speeded through her lips, and as one of her hands moved spasmodically her nail grazed a male nipple.

With a strength she did not perceive at the moment, his hands dug into the soft flesh of her arms and pulled her forward, the upper curve of her breasts revealed by her bikini top tingling from contact with his heaving chest. Her nipples began to tauten and her breath mingled with the labored air that escaped his parted lips. As he drew her inexorably closer she looked into eyes now darkened with passion. His head moved with a maddening slowness to close the gap between their mouths. Her own hands went up his chest, her long, slender fingers burying themselves in the golden mat, whether to stop him or to encourage him, she was no longer sure.

But he suddenly stiffened and lifted his head just as his warm, minty breath caressed her open, welcoming lips. Dale could feel him forcibly gain control of himself, removing the heat of his loins from her pelvis, and then he released her and stepped away.

Surprised and slightly unsteady, Dale also moved backward, and felt something give under her foot.

She quickly lifted her left leg, but not before something sticky was plastered thoroughly onto the sole of her foot.

She put her arm on the wall to keep her balance and looked down, the wheels of her mind still not spinning rapidly but stuck in low gear, her physical yearning taking drugging precedence.

Burke seemed to recover quickly. He finished pulling on his T-shirt, which barely reached his hips, and she noticed that his blue shorts were so abbreviated that they resembled a G-string.

When Burke knelt, his head only an inch away from her appendix scar, Dale backed away in alarm. But her hasty motion was arrested when Burke seized her leg and picked up an object that squished as he grabbed it.

Dale tentatively pulled on her leg and breathed an inner sigh of relief when Burke released it. He rose, carrying all of her violently discarded articles, his face once more in the relatively safer vicinity of hers and not near the stomach that had quivered at his closeness, and the exposed, sensitive navel that had been tickled erotically by his expelled breath.

"Here you are," he said, offering her her possessions.

Dale accepted them stonily, still trying to tame her racing heart into submission and her liquefied limbs into flesh and solid bone. The books, glasses, and lotion clutched protectively against her chest, she looked at Burke's left hand, where a tube of lotion lay like a ravished earthworm in the broad palm.

"Coconut oil," he explained. Dale raised her eyes to meet Burke's amused gaze. "This is what I was coming to your bedroom to offer. I wanted to make sure that creamy skin was properly protected."

"'Beware of Greeks bearing gifts,'" she said, thankful that her power of speech had been restored. Still, it sounded as rusty as the souped-up car she'd inherited in high school from her older brother. "I suppose your thoughtfulness included an offer to spread it on my tender skin?"

Burke's smile was boyish. "Mother may have raised a forward boy—never a stupid one."

Dale, still smarting from his superior control of his emotions, tended to agree that she was the stupid one for almost succumbing to the enticement of a gorgeous male body, a fact that called for an immediate implementation of her plan.

"Well, as you can see, I've come prepared." She held up her lotion and smiled with a hint of malice. "I guess your strategy didn't work this time, Burke Sheridan."

"Strategy?" he inquired innocently.

Waving her lotion in his face, she taunted, "I guess you'll be the one who'll suffer now. It may be a pleasure to see you roasting in the sun."

Burke shook his head in mocking admonishment. "I never would have figured you as vindictive." Rubbing his palm on his upper thigh, he added, "But you'll be disappointed. I've roasted in deserts and beaches in one-hundred-degree-plus heat. My hide is pretty thick, so I won't burn."

Her eyes were attracted to the golden-brown strip of skin visible between T-shirt and trunks, and then were helplessly drawn to his hand resting so near the prominent bulge outlined by the stretch material. Dale fervently wished he *would* burn—as intensely as he was making her sizzle now.

Dragging her gaze from the section of his anatomy that was indelibly ingrained in her memory but that still commanded her visual attention like a magnet, she realized he'd spoken again.

"Wh-what?"

"I said you'd better put on your screening cream soon. You look like you're suffering from third-degree burns."

Dale gave him a frigid smile. "Very funny." She didn't bother looking down at herself, knowing he was undoubtedly right. She pushed away from the wall, intent on escaping his unendurable presence, and slipped on the cream smeared on the floor.

Burke's arm curled about her waist, preventing an ignominious fall, but Dale was not up to appreciating his opportune help. Obviously, he was aware of it, because his arm left her waist once he was sure she had her footing.

Feeling obliged to express her gratitude out of inbred etiquette if nothing else, Dale forced the words out past stiff lips.

"Thank you."

"Brrr," Burke said, his body doing a sensual imitation of a shiver. "It's positively glacial all of a sudden."

"Think of it as a substitute for a cold shower," she told him, looking pointedly at the blue briefs, which was once more stretched to its limit. "You need it."

As she swept haughtily past him, glad that *she* had silenced *him* for once, her dignified exit was somewhat marred by further slips on her greasy foot. The squish-squashing sounds of her footsteps on deck were accompanied by a strange low rumble that reverberated against her bare back.

Thoroughly incensed, but not about to give Burke the satisfaction of turning around and losing her precarious hold on her temper, Dale marched like a soldier into battle, feeling his body heat like a furnace that warmed her back and buttocks as he trailed her closely. She wondered silently whether the insensitive, exasperating oaf could actually be laughing at her expense.

When she emerged into sunlight, she didn't have to guess any more. The choked, strangled noises erupting from Burke's tanned throat turned into gusty laughter, and as he proceeded to gather his fishing equipment, his shoulders shook under the material lovingly detailing their muscular breadth.

Shaking off her somnolence, Dale rose from the yellow lounge chair in the sun deck. She stretched and looked about her, as she'd done periodically over the past hour to allay any suspicions Burke might harbor. Professedly taking in the beauty of the peaceful afternoon, she pivoted slowly and inhaled the fresh summer air.

Her skin had begun to tingle, a sure sign that sunburn was imminent. She placed a bookmark in her novel, which she could just not concentrate on, and placed it on the chair along with another novel. Going to the side of the boat, she leaned over the railing and looked the length of the *Seaprincess,* lazily studying its pleasing lines, the soft pastels of blue and yellow among the predominant white a soothing sight.

Casually, she sauntered to the opposite side, where she knew Burke was fishing. At least, that had been his stated intention. Although he'd started out in an alert, sitting position, he was now lying on a large boulder that protruded over the iridescent waters. A shabby straw hat covered his face, and his hands were resting on his lap, holding an immobile fishing rod.

She made a production of touching the tender skin on her shoulder, not having to feign a wince. If he was awake, he would see that her delicate skin was already screaming for release from the sun. Picking up the tube she'd placed on the railing after putting on some lotion, Dale applied some more now. As she put it on, rubbing it in delicately, she shook her head, thinking that despite all the meetings she'd planned and conventions she'd organized in places like California and Florida, she'd never been able to enjoy the lovely settings. The bulk of her work had to be done indoors—in her office, on planes, inside hotels—and she was too busy arranging such activities as golf, tennis, and poolside parties to participate in them.

As she took another casual look at Burke, Dale again despaired at how close to shore he had anchored the *Seaprincess*. She'd have felt a lot better if she'd been in the middle of the wide river, several yards rather than mere feet away.

But she was not likely to get another opportunity, so she had to take advantage of this one now. She pushed her silver-lensed glasses, which were sliding down her perspiring nose, back up, and noticed that her hands were trembling.

Throwing the tube onto the lounge chair, Dale took a leisurely stroll toward the steel ladder and, just as she was about to step onto the first rung, cast another glance at Burke. Then, without breaking stride, she completed her descent.

Burke was still in the same prone position he'd held for the past half-hour, giving every indication of being sound asleep. Of course, there was no way to make sure. She could only hope that even if he was only dozing, he would not realize what she was up to before she was safely away.

Sneaking one last, uneasy look, Dale saw that he hadn't moved. Quickly, she headed for the wheel and turned on the engine.

After a couple of false starts, it purred to life, and Dale ejected her pent-up breath. Just as she was about to shift to full speed, she remembered something: the anchor!

She pressed the button to retrieve it, then went back to the wheel, gripping it with moist, clammy hands that were made even more slippery from the residue of suntan lotion. Hastily rubbing her hands on the minuscule bikini bottom, she cursed her lack of foresight in not bringing a towel with her.

As she began to guide the *Seaprincess* forward, Dale noticed that her hands were shaking. You fool, she berated herself, but she couldn't escape the fact that she felt guilty as hell for leaving Burke behind. And what was worse, she experienced not only guilt but also a sense of desolation. She'd known Burke Sheridan for less than a day, and already she was reluctant to have him out of her life!

Dale felt torn in two.

One part of her demanded that she turn back, while the other part vociferously warned that she was losing all objectivity. A few caresses and expert flirting were threatening her resolution of two years before. And she was an expert on charm and its lack of substance.

But even as the voice of reason told her that this had all been a game to Burke, a virile man who obviously enjoyed women and could not pass them up any more than a child could pass up licorice in a candy store, Dale felt the bitter taste of regret. Burke, of course, would come to no harm. She'd call Wyatt Martin as soon as she was a few more miles away—the *Seaprincess* had been built for comfort but certainly not speed—and would ask him to send someone to pick Burke up. Once back at the Sapphire Marina, Burke could resume his vacation on another boat, if one was available. And if one wasn't, then he'd just have to make do and spend the rest of his vacation fishing from a dock.

Sternly quieting her conflicting inner voices, Dale kept her errant hand from shifting into reverse and gripped the steering wheel so hard that her knuckles turned white. She concentrated her attention on piloting the houseboat and tried to appreciate the open beauty of the mighty Mississippi.

"Going somewhere?"

- 4 -

SHIVERS CLIMBED UP her spine at the husky words. Dale shut off the motor and turned to face the music.

Burke stood a few feet away, his deep chest heaving, his wet hair plastered to his broad forehead. As his gaze locked with hers, she saw that he was absolutely furious. Although the shivers of trepidation increased, Dale tried to keep her uneasiness from showing in her eyes. After what seemed like eons to her but must have been only seconds, Burke moved. Slowly, lazily, inexorably.

Her heart dislodged from her own heaving chest and filled her mouth; yet, Dale stood her ground. She wasn't sure what retaliation he would seek, but she didn't intend to show fear. What bothered her the most in the turmoil of emotions she was experiencing was the severe control he was exerting over his, and the flicker of an unreadable emotion in the angry blue irises. Disappointment?

She wasn't sure and was given no more time to decipher his feelings, for Burke moved swiftly and deceptively, and she found herself in his arms. Knowing that at five eleven she was no lightweight, she was stunned that he could pick her up so easily and carry her so effortlessly.

Her own arms crept instinctively around his neck, and even in her predicament, she could feel the sensual tug of his virility, his body warm and wet and hard against her bare, fear-chilled skin, his male smell combined with fresh river scents, clean and intoxicating.

Her unease began to be slowly joined by other emotions, and the feral light in his eyes told her Burke was aware of it seconds before a half-smile played about his firm, sensual lips, and his gaze dropped to a bust that rose and fell in response to his raw appeal.

He stopped and extended his arms over the rail, but Dale resisted the instinctive urge to tighten her hold. If he wanted to give her a taste of her own medicine and abandon her as she'd planned to do with him, there was nothing she could do. The self-defense lessons she'd taken would not serve her in her present position—and if she were dropped overboard, she'd at least keep her pride and dignity.

"Doesn't feel very good, does it?" Burke asked, his lazy drawl grating on her skin, his arms stretching out even farther. She would have preferred some old-fashioned cussing—not this total control Burke was exhibiting over himself. She certainly would be using a few choice expressions herself if the positions were reversed. The smile curving his lips widened, and his teeth gleamed white against the sun-browned skin. "If you apologize nicely, I might let you stay on."

Dale's dark head snapped up proudly, her chin

lifting with determination. "Your arms would fall off before I did. I still think you were wrong in insisting on staying, knowing my circumstances. And I'd try it again if I could . . . but hopefully with better results."

His eyes flashed for an instant, and then the blue-green fire died as he said insinuatingly, "Maybe you can persuade me to let you stay some other way."

Dale read the intent in his eyes, and the embryonic stirrings of passion she'd felt dissolved as the first snowflakes of the season on summer-warmed ground. When his mouth descended on hers, she moved her head aside, and his lips brushed against her cheek. Expecting him to persist, Dale was surprised when he didn't try to kiss her again.

Distrusting him, she pivoted her head slowly, cautiously. Raising her eyes to meet his, her glance traveled past the strong brown column of his neck, where his dark blond hair curled damply; the square jaw, already showing a five-o'clock shadow; the firm male mouth curved in a smile . . .

A smile! He was actually smiling! Her gaze flew to his, at first darkening to jade with shocked surprise, then turning golden-green with rage as she saw the mocking glint in his.

"No go, right?" he asked, amusement threading the deep, rich voice.

"Put me down!" she demanded.

He didn't release her, and when she began to struggle in his arms, he merely tightened his grip, holding her close against his body. "Had you scared there for a minute, didn't I?"

Dale's generous mouth thinned in anger. She had been scared all right—but for a different reason than the one he obviously assumed. In that instant when his head had lowered, she'd felt an aching stab of disappointment, thinking that maybe she'd misjudged him all along. Why such a possibility disturbed her, she didn't want to consider at the moment. She only knew that during the past twenty-four hours she'd come to know and like him, even though she'd fought the attraction. She had not been afraid of him harming her or forcing her—merely of his proving himself to be a different man than she'd judged.

"Don't you think you'd better put me down?" she asked him, ignoring his question altogether. "I'm not exactly feather-light."

"That you're not," he agreed quickly—too quickly for her taste. "But you're in luck. I've never gone in for model types. I've always preferred the more endowed specimens."

"I'm in luck!"

The gleam of laughter in his eyes increased at her indignation. That wonderful rumble began in his chest again, moving to his shoulders, which began to shake with laughter. His laughter increased the friction of skin upon skin, and when she saw Burke's method of retaliation contained that element of playfulness always near the surface, Dale felt her own indignation begin to dissipate. She looked into the brilliant opalescent eyes that squinted under the glare of the sun, and as spasms shook his body she felt a smile tug at her own lips. The sudden thought hit her that yes, it *had* been disappointment she'd read in his eyes. Apparently, he'd also formed a lightning-quick opinion of her, and had been reluctant to have his judgment proved wrong. Male vanity, she dismissed swiftly, attempting to get out of the uncomfortably delightful prison of his arms.

When Burke wouldn't release her, she redoubled her kicking. Her efforts, coupled with the unsteadiness his own laughter induced, made Burke rock on his feet. He tried to steady himself, but she increased her wriggling, and all of a sudden he started to tip backward.

Dale sensed the imminent fall the instant he did and could have attempted to counterbalance him by shifting her weight, but with malicious glee she pressed herself against his body with such force that he fell flat on his back, her not inconsiderable weight landing so hard on him that she squeezed his breath out temporarily.

When she tried to scramble to her feet, however, his left arm snaked out and wrapped about her waist, impeding her movement. Dale pushed against his chest, but by now Burke had recovered his wind, and his right hand came up to cradle the back of her head, tangling in the gently waving strands.

"That wasn't very nice," he murmured huskily, but there was no rancor in his lazy glance. Dale suddenly became aware of the intimacy of their positions, her slender length fitted perfectly to his solid, muscular frame, her nipples hardening from the cold wetness of his T-shirt.

But the combined warmth of their bodies soon dispelled any chills, and her breasts swelled as he crushed their softness to the hard planes of his chest, their peaks pulsating from the sensual contact. His eyes caressed her lips seconds before his mouth claimed them, covering the soft, full curves with a hunger that found an echoing response in her.

His lips tasted and savored hers, learned their shape and texture, teasing first one corner, then the other,

covering and retreating until Dale thought she'd go
mad if she didn't have the full possession of his mouth.
Sucking her lower lip into his mouth, Burke nibbled
it gently, expertly, until a low murmur rose in her
throat and was diffused against his mouth. He reacted
by tightening his hold on her, but he kept teasing her
mouth in a way that made arrows of need shoot to
her very center, inflaming all nerve centers in their
path.

Her mind dazed with the heady fumes of desire,
Dale couldn't comprehend how Burke could exact
such a response from her. When he relaxed her lower
lip and licked her mouth with the tip of his tongue in
ever-widening erotic circles, she dug her fingers in
his thick gold hair, bringing his head closer to hers
to force him to complete their kiss.

Burke pressed the rough, velvety tip of his tongue
between her lips, and she parted them eagerly. But
he still didn't satisfy her wordless request. His tongue
glided over her teeth, savoring their pearly smoothness, and then brushed against the underside of her
lips. He lifted his mouth just a fraction to allow them
to inhale a much needed gulp of fresh, flower-scented
air, then covered her mouth once more, his tongue
plunging inside the moist recesses with a consuming
eroticism that made everything go black for a second.

Dale closed her eyes as his hot, demanding mouth
worked on hers and she gave herself to his sweet
torment. He drank from the honeyed richness of her
mouth, his tongue engaging hers in a velvety duel that
had them straining toward each other, both seeking a
more complete, more satisfactory union.

His left hand left her waist to skim a path of fire
along the sensitive ridge of her back, slowly and gently

trailing her vertebrae with callused fingertips until they came to rest on the back clasp of her bikini top. As his deft, sure fingers disposed of the fastening, Dale stiffened. Her spiraling senses began a sharp descent as she became fully cognizant once again.

How could she have let this happen? She must be crazy! She had just met Burke—and had recognized him immediately for what he was. Yet, here she'd let herself get carried away—and she was no novice when it came to disillusionment.

Trying to control her jagged breathing, Dale pushed away from Burke frantically.

At first, she was afraid he wouldn't release her. His eyes were glazed, a dark flush rode high on his angular cheekbones, and his arms tightened instinctively around her. But when she increased the pressure against his slick, warm shoulders, the film of passion was erased from his eyes and they regained their usual sharpness and alertness. He crushed her against him one last time, molding her soft curves to his muscular body so closely that she felt the outline of his hardened manhood hotly delineated between her trembling thighs. He breathed deeply, and a convulsive shudder shook his large frame just as he released her, gently depositing her on deck. He rose to his feet and pulled her up in one smooth motion.

The rueful look in his eyes made her feel doubly guilty. Although she didn't believe it was the sole province of the woman to check passion and dictate standards of behavior, in this case she felt she'd been remiss. After telling Burke so emphatically that she did not want involvement of any kind, she'd let herself go as if there were no tomorrow.

"I'm sorry," she began, determined to take responsibility for her actions.

He leaned against the railing, the powerful muscles of his thighs in sharp relief as his back arched backward. "About stopping? No more so than I."

"About even letting you get started."

"I thought I detected some cooperation." His smile flashed again, slow and sexy, and she ran her hands nervously over her thighs. His interested glance followed.

"It was too much to hope for that you'd overlook my momentary aberration—"

"Overlook? Lady, you made my day."

She sighed. "You're certainly making it hard for me to apologize."

"Why should I make it easier? I should have thrown you overboard."

"Why didn't you?"

When he didn't answer right away, she crossed her arms over her chest. His gaze followed again. Frustrated, she dropped her arms and laced them in front of her. When his glance dropped, she realized her clenched hands were lying right over the minute triangle of her bikini bottoms. She crossed her arms again.

He finally relented, and the glitter in the teal-blue eyes softened to a low gleam. His tone was sober when he said, "I almost did. I was expecting a move like this."

Her eyes widened and he grinned wolfishly.

"You don't think I'd choose this godforsaken spot for fishing? There are plenty of fish in other sections and tributaries. I just wanted to test my theory. And if you did try something, I wanted to make sure I'd be able to counter your move."

She bit her lip and turned sideways so he wouldn't see her consternation. But she couldn't totally keep the bitterness from her voice.

"I'm glad I provided some amusement for you. Too bad I had to play when the cards were stacked against me."

He straightened and pulled her around to face him.

"Hey, don't make me feel guilty. You wanted to make me shark bait."

Her eyebrows curved. "I didn't realize there were sharks in these waters." She paused a minute, then added deliberately. "Unless you mean the two-legged variety."

"Would you have really gone through with it?"

She didn't flinch. "I thought I had."

He dropped his arm and turned to look at the sky, which was fast becoming overcast. "It's going to rain soon. I'll go find us a sheltered cove."

She stopped him as he passed in front of her.

"You didn't answer my question," she reminded him. "Why didn't you throw me overboard?"

He looked at her, his expression serious. "I understood how you felt, your need for solitude and privacy. It just so happened that this time I also needed some time away before returning to my job, and our needs collided. If I'd been in your place, I'd probably have done the same thing."

She let go of his arm and said, "Thank you. That was kind and gentlemanly of you."

"I'm neither kind nor a gentleman. I do appreciate guts and honesty, and you have plenty of those, lady."

"Dale."

"Dale." His mouth twitched.

"Ah . . . about the other . . ."

"You mean about getting so carried away in my arms that you almost let me take you?"

She breathed deeply and counted to ten. "I'd like to be able to fling an accusation at you, but unfortunately the only thing you did was take advantage of the situation. I did provide cooperation. It won't happen again."

"Not until you approach me again," he agreed.

He walked toward the wheel and she followed him. "You mean *unless* I approach you."

He turned the full power of his gaze on her. "You're as attracted to me as I am to you. And there's nothing more sexy to a man than a woman who's imagined him as a sexual partner."

With that, he turned his full attention to the rapidly darkening sky. The wind had picked up, and now the Mississippi waters were churning like a witches' brew.

Knowing he was right didn't make the pill easier to swallow. Dale turned to go and change, but he said, "Wait! Look up ahead."

She did, but couldn't distinguish anything of great import. She noticed the tenseness of his body, though, and as the boat's aluminum hull cut through the rippling waters, Dale saw what Burke had spied crucial moments before.

A large log had collided with a submerged stump and now blocked their path. Burke checked for oncoming craft, but luckily the commercial traffic that had abounded earlier in the day had passed them and they still had this portion of the river to themselves, so Burke could maneuver the large boat easily.

"See the color of the water?" he asked. Dale noticed it had become browner, swirls of yellow indicating silt. "You're seeing a unique phenomenon: flocculation," he told her.

"Flocculation?" Dale repeated, holding her breath as Burke skillfully steered the *Seaprincess* past the obstruction.

"The current carries these floccules—masses of viscid mud, fifteen feet deep sometimes—which can clog water strainers and cause considerable damage to shafts and strut bearings."

As they cleared the danger spot, Dale released her pent-up breath in a relieved whoosh. She wanted to tell him how impressed she'd been with his cool handling of the situation, and realized how lucky it was she hadn't managed to dislodge Burke from the boat.

But she still felt awkward around him—and awkward with herself. She'd led a very quiet social life since her break-up with Joel, and her lack of self-control both scared her and made her feel embarrassed.

As she turned to go once more, Burke said softly, "Dale?"

She waited but didn't turn around.

"Do you see why I couldn't let you get away with it? By coming on board last night and spiriting you away, I prevented you from getting the orientation you needed to survive on the river alone. I would have been responsible if anything had happened to you."

She didn't say anything, feeling like a perfect stinker. But he wasn't finished.

"And please, don't feel self-conscious about what happened. I know I promised to behave and haven't exactly been keeping that promise. But I had no idea of what would happen between us." She turned at this and met his gaze. It was rueful and self-mocking. "Believe me," he said, "it hit me like a ton of bricks, too."

She smiled; a heavy weight had been plucked from her shoulders. "And I apologize for trying to leave you behind," she said graciously.

"But only because it was a sneaky thing to do."

"Had I been able to throw you overboard—"

"I know, I know. The disadvantages of being a frail female."

She laughed, and his eyes roved quickly over her figure. "Although I must say," he drawled, "the female body has powers that cannot be duplicated by male ones. You left me practically incapacitated out there."

She remembered his high state of arousal and told him, "You asked for that. Maybe next time you'll be more of a gentleman with a helpless female."

He snorted. "I don't suppose I can get your promise that you won't try to get rid of me again."

"After how dangerous you've proven to be—in more ways than one?"

He grinned. "I guess I'll just have to keep a sharp lookout."

Her eyes returned his lecherous once-over, and she told him as she headed for the bedroom, "You do that. But don't forget to find us a safe harbor."

- 5 -

THE HEAVY STORM buffeted the *Seaprincess* as Dale lay in her bed. She hooked the pillow between her wrist and elbow to be able to look out the small window better.

It was a doozy of a storm: the jagged streaks of lightning clawed at the onyx sky with speedy regularity, and the rhythmic music of the rain beat upon the metal with great insistence. The air smelled wonderfully fresh and springlike, and the cacophony of sounds above and below and around her was strangely soothing. She'd always liked storms, and as she lay watching the awesome display, snug in her one flannel nightgown under the crisp cotton sheets, Dale thought nothing could have been more perfect.

Well, almost. The thought of another warm body sharing the sheets with her—particularly a teal-blue-eyed six footer—did have a lot of merit. But realizing that fantasy would bring nothing but trouble. She'd already courted trouble today, and once was enough. Dale thought of herself as a person who learned from her mistakes, and Burke flashed trouble in neon signs.

She settled deeper into the mattress, sighing with pleasure. Actually, a houseboat would be an ideal setting for a small, high-level meeting. Executives often had difficulty trying to make time in their busy schedules to discuss potential mergers and acquisitions. A weekend on a houseboat, one sleeping six or eight, would give them uninterrupted time for sensitive negotiations.

She was already outlining in her mind several points of the proposal she intended to present to her boss upon her return to work when a heavy pounding on the door made her jump in bed.

"Awake in there?" Burke growled.

"If I wasn't, I'd certainly be by now," she replied tartly. "Your knocking would awaken the dead."

The door opened and Burke walked in unceremoniously. "Remember that movie *Night of the Living Dead?* It was—"

"Please, don't remind me," she cut in, moving her legs out of the way as he perched on the side of her bed. "That was one of the worst films I've ever seen. Why it became a cult classic is beyond me."

"People love movies that terrify them and appeal to their basic instincts. Remember the part when the truck explodes and the zombies get to it—"

"Will you stop it?" she asked him, shuddering. As he leaned forward in a threatening manner, she asked him suspiciously, "Have you been drinking?"

Laughing, he put his arms on each side of her. "You sure are a hard person to scare. Here I thought you'd be shaking in terror from that loud storm, and you were just lying there looking as calm and comfy as can be." He leaned toward her a bit more. "And as delicious, delectable, appetizing..."

"Would you mind getting off those adjectives? Particularly after the movie we were just discussing."

"But I can't help it. That long, slender, creamy neck is just irresistible—"

"You have the wrong monster. Those are vampires."

"Your arm doesn't look so bad either," he said, swooping down and closing his teeth about the flesh of her upper arm.

She didn't cringe. Unobtrusively, she moved her hand to his knee and found the spot she wanted. Then she squeezed.

Burke jumped off the bed as if he'd been shot.

"What the hell...? What did you do to me?"

"Just practiced self-defense. My older brother, Roy, taught me a few tricks when some other boys in the neighborhood ganged up on me."

His mind zeroed in on one word. "Roy?"

She sighed. "Yes. We were named after Roy Rogers and Dale Evans. They were favorites of my parents."

He didn't laugh, but as he sat cautiously on the edge of the bed he said, "I guess it's better than Chip and Dale."

Resignedly, Dale told him, "My brother's nickname is Chip."

This time he did laugh, and was promptly hit with a pillow, which he returned with lightning-quick reflexes. A free-for-all ensued, and when there were no more pillows and sheets to be thrown, Burke collapsed on the bed.

They remained quiet for a moment, their silence fraught with sexual tension, but not an uncomfortable one. Dale felt she knew Burke a bit better, and she trusted him. At least, she trusted him enough to know that he wouldn't try anything in the bedroom, where it would be too easy to get carried away. She was convinced he wouldn't want to take the element of choice away from her.

"Would you believe I came in here to ask you something?" he said.

"Sure I would. A man who worries about my safety and who's too much of a gentleman to throw me overboard or to force a seduction must have some integrity."

"I told you, I am no gentleman."

"Sorry. I didn't mean to tarnish your image."

He smiled, the slow smile that made her blood race and her head feel giddy.

"You're one difficult woman."

"I aim to please."

"If that's the case..." He moved forward a few inches.

"I have a few more tricks up my sleeve," she warned him, smiling sweetly. He paused with exaggerated alarm, and she laughed. "What did you want to ask me?"

"If you wanted to have a barbecue."

"Sure. When?"

"Right now."

"Right *now?*"

"Why not? I doubt either of us will get much sleep, and I'm starving."

Now that he had mentioned it, Dale realized she felt kind of hungry herself. Thoughts of outdoor cooking always had a strong effect on her appetite.

"A big, juicy steak, corn on the cob, potatoes baked in their own skin and smothered with sour cream . . ."

"All right, all right. You've gotten my juices flowing."

He was on her in a flash. "I'll substitute culinary words for amorous nothings in your ear," he told her as he let his weight fall over her.

She pushed at his shoulders, laughing. "Get off me, Tarzan. You must weigh a ton."

"Such irreverence to the cook. That may mean starvation, woman." But he did get off her, and Dale chided herself silently for the disappointment she felt.

"But I'm the cook, remember?" she told him. "I promised you a barbecue. That is, if we can get a fire started in this downpour."

"I worked in Asia for a while, and if I can get a fire started in those monsoons, I can get one going in a small deluge like this one." He got up and walked to the door. "You'd better put on something warm. Do you have any boots?"

She shook her head, a bit dazed at the prospect of a midnight dinner. And a barbecue in the middle of the rain, at that!

"Then I'll lend you mine."

"But what about you?" she asked.

"I've got a tough hide, remember?"

He did it. By stretching and tying some canvas between two young trees, Burke secured a dry space for them. Dale got a fire started, and they were soon enjoying their steaks, corn, and potatoes.

"Want some more corn?" Burke asked as he peeled the husk from his third cob.

"No, thanks. I think I've had enough," Dale replied, patting her satiated stomach.

She watched him as he sank his strong teeth into the tender kernels, and saw the light of the campfire dash about his features, making him look younger.

He put a dollop of sour cream on the last remaining potato, and she had to smile at his voracious appetite.

"You're one terrific cook," he said. Before biting into the potato, he asked. "Sure you don't want any more?"

"Positive. You go ahead. You seem to need it more than I."

"Maybe because I do all the running."

"Your attention and compliments have been duly noted and appreciated. You can quit your pursuit now," Dale told him dryly.

"Lady, if it were only that simple."

Dale moved restlessly against the young tree she was leaning on and said sharply, "Would you stop calling me *lady?*"

"Can't." He finished the corn and threw the husk in the fire. "I can't seem to get that song, 'Lay, Lady, Lay,' out of my head when you're around."

Suddenly uncomfortable, Dale rose and began to gather up the remnants of their impromptu midnight barbecue.

"If that's the way you're going to behave, we may as well go back to the houseboat," she said.

"I brought sleeping bags. I thought we might spend the night here."

"Under the stars?" she asked wryly, to hide the appeal the idea held for her. There might not be a starry firmament above, but she held fond memories of all the times her family had gone camping, and as a teenager she'd dreamed about being able to share a tent someday with the man of her dreams. She'd since outgrown such adolescent fantasies, but the magic of the outdoors had never died for her.

"Well?" he asked her as she put their trash into a large brown paper bag.

"Promise to keep to your own sleeping bag?"

"Solemnly."

Dale shook her head, smiling, and put an old pot on the fire. "Where did you get this relic?" she asked him as she put some milk in her cup.

He looked up from the sleeping bag he was unrolling. "I bought that a few years back. It seems indestructible. I take it with me wherever I go; it's sort of a talisman," he told her, dragging the sleeping bags near the fire.

"Don't tell me you plan to put them in the fire to warm them. Were you one of those children that put goldfish in the oven to dry because they looked so cold and wet?"

"My, you really come alive after twelve," he said, leaving the small circle of light and warmth.

He came back a few minutes later, his wet hair clinging to his forehead, his sweater plastered to his powerful chest. He was still barefoot and carrying a large log.

"Aren't you afraid of catching cold?" she asked him, her natural concern aroused.

"I told you, I'm pretty tough, and I'm used to conditions a lot worse than this." He set the log near the fire and arranged the sleeping bags near it. "We can use this as a headrest."

Dale nodded and checked the pot. The water was almost boiling. "Do you want milk in your coffee?"

"No, thanks." His words came out muffled, and Dale automatically turned toward him. Her eyes widened appreciatively at the sight of the beautifully contoured shoulders and golden chest hair that gleamed in the firelight. As his head emerged from the wet sweater he was taking off, she turned her gaze away.

"Were *you* one of those children that put goldfish in the oven?" he asked suddenly.

Her head pivoted back to him and she laughed. "Nope. That was Chip. He's only fifteen months older than I, and used to be a holy terror."

She checked the water again and heard the sound of a zipper being opened. She didn't turn her head this time.

"I suppose you were a perfect angel," Burke said.

"No, I suppose I had my moments," she admitted, smiling. Amusing memories flooded her mind, and she forgot about his state of undress as she asked, "What about you? Do you have any brothers or sisters?"

This time his lower torso came into view, and she saw that at least he had some briefs on. They were a vibrant shade of red, and she couldn't resist teasing him. "A Valentine's Day present?"

"A present, anyway," he agreed, coming over to check the pot. "I think the water's ready."

Dale put instant coffee in both cups, and Burke filled them with steaming water.

She couldn't keep her eyes from the stretchy red material of his briefs. He caught her looking, and despite her embarrassment, she brazened it out. "They certainly are . . . colorful," she remarked.

"You know, the human male is unlike the males of other species. We don't come with vibrant, eye-catching plumage. We have to make the best of what we've got to attract the females."

"With your body, your face, and your hair, you are a standout anywhere, honey," she told him throatily.

He gave a playful tug at the long braid that flowed down her back. "Smartmouth."

He was sitting cross-legged on his sleeping bag, and Dale felt cold just looking at him. "Aren't you somewhat . . . chilly . . . like that?" she asked.

His body shuddered in a sensual shiver. "As cold as ice. Come here and warm me."

"You never stop, do you?"

"You're a poet's inspiration, la—Dale."

Smiling, she went to sit on her own checkered sleeping bag, which he'd placed only an inch away from his.

"Do you always bring two sleeping bags along— just in case?"

He took a sip of hot coffee. "These are Martin's. I've come alone on my last two trips."

"That's right. You mentioned you needed rest on occasion. I guess you don't get much of it if you bring a woman. I imagine you go on overdrive."

"I suppose you mean because my job isolates me from women—and consequently from sexual opportunities—for long stretches. You're oversimplifying, Dale. I do miss women—I like them, but not just as convenient bed partners. Although you may find it hard to believe, I don't come on like this to every woman I meet."

"Just to every blonde, redhead, and brunette."

"You've got the coloring reversed. I prefer brunettes."

"What do you know? A man of discerning tastes."

He looked at her over the cup he was drinking from. "Are you really this cynical, or are you just afraid to let someone in close?"

Dale tried to feel upset at him for trying to break through her defenses, but realized she didn't have all her barriers up tonight. Or perhaps he'd been chipping away at the mortar so effectively that he'd made a crack without her knowing it.

"You must admit, you've come on rather strong," she told him.

"Only because if I didn't, you'd crawl into your shell even more."

That angered her. "I thought you said I turned you on because I'd indicated I was attracted to you."

He finished drinking and put his cup on the ground. "And you'd rather have chicken pox, right?"

She didn't deny it. She wasn't proud of her lack of indifference around him. Once burned, twice shy, after all. And she suspected an involvement with Burke would consume her in its conflagration.

He seemed to take her silence for confirmation and didn't say anything for a while. Dale sipped slowly from her cup, unaware that her coffee had already become cold. When the cup was empty, she automatically put it on the ground next to her and curled her legs, hugging them and resting her chin on her knees.

The night sounds were muted, the occasional call of wildlife and the susurration of the river reaching them faintly underneath the soft, steady patter of the rain.

Watching the flames that licked and devoured the logs and twigs they'd gathered, Dale felt her muscles unwind, and her mind relaxed from its constant analyzing. Burke had set up camp in a small clearing near shore, and the orange-blue flames created dancing images on the craggy bluffs that bordered one side of the mysterious emerald splendor.

She forced her eyes away from the woods and stole a glance at Burke, who was now lying on top of his sleeping bag, his body bronzed and muscular and relaxed, gleaming in the flickering firelight with the polish of good health and hard work. He looked all too dangerously appealing; yet, somehow Dale couldn't tear her gaze away.

He turned his head and fixed her with a glittering stare. "You never did answer my question," he said softly.

"You mean the one about my preferring to have chickenpox?" She knew very well that he meant the other question, about her being afraid to let anyone get too close. But she hardly cared to tell him about Joel. Instead, she went on, "I think we've talked enough about me tonight. Why don't we discuss you for a change?"

He seemed to hesitate for a moment, and Dale realized he was reticent to discuss himself. Like her, Burke was a very private person who didn't like to give people deep glimpses into himself.

With one quick, smooth motion he was in his sleeping bag, and then he was resting on his elbow, facing her, that wonderful, gleaming bronze torso still in display as the cover slipped to his waist.

"Why don't you get under the covers? The rain will be stopping soon and it'll be getting chilly."

She dragged her eyes away from his body. It was an effort. Like any normal woman, she was attracted to a powerful, fit masculine shape, but this was ridiculous. Her eyes seemed to have a will of their own since alighting upon him that first time, which now seemed ages ago.

Unlike Burke, she didn't take off her royal-blue sweater or navy slacks. She removed Burke's boots, which fitted like boats, and placed them on the ground near the fire. Then she turned to face him, making a concentrated effort to keep her gaze on his face.

"So tell me, how did you get into engineering?"

His slow grin turned her stomach to melted butter.

"Are you operating on the assumption that talk is safer than action?"

"Not necessarily. After all, you did barge into my life. If I'm going to be around you for the next few days, I'd like to know something about you."

His body went oddly still. "Does that mean there'll be no further attempts at mutiny?"

"I wouldn't go that far. I see us as co-captains. I won't try to leave you behind, but I'm certainly not going to follow blindly whatever direction you give me."

He grinned. "That's good enough for me. I won't have to spend sleepless nights now, imagining myself abandoned."

"I can't see you spending sleepless nights over anything," she scoffed. "Besides, you managed to outmaneuver me, and I'm not very proud of myself."

"For trying to get rid of me or for getting caught?"

"Both. I'll make the best of it, but I really did need some time on my own."

"Some man pressuring you to go to bed?"

His comment was so out of left field that she stared at him for a moment, speechless. The gentle tapping of the rain on the canvas roof over their heads filled the sudden silence. Dale needlessly rearranged her sleeping bag over the plastic Burke had spread under their bags as she debated whether or not to answer him. She finally decided to, thinking that it might be better to give him an inkling of what made her tick.

"Why do you think some man would have to pressure me?"

"Because you're one hell of a sexy lady, but that doesn't necessarily mean you're not selective. I imagine in your job you have to beat them down with sticks."

She laughed, the clear tinkling sound carrying in the pure night air. "I'd like to do exactly that with some of the more obnoxious conventioneers. But I'm stuck with diplomatic methods, unless I want to be out of a job soon."

"Does that mean I don't get an answer?"

"It means I think you're being very personal, but no, I'm not on this boat to escape from a man. I have a job decision to make."

"Thinking of changing professions?"

"No. I love what I do. But I've been offered a position in St. Louis, which will mean a bit more travel and more responsibility. The responsibility I can handle, but I've recently bought a house, which I've been decorating. I get to travel plenty as it is on my job, and I don't want that part to increase. I'm somewhat tired of hotel rooms and food on the road."

He nodded thoughtfully. "All your friends and family are in Iowa?"

"Most of them. Chip's in the Air Force, so I see him only occasionally."

"So basically it's a question of deciding between a new, higher-paying job that may provide you with greater professional satisfaction, or a safe, comfortable job where you can set down roots and stagnate?"

She laughed a bit uneasily. "Do you have anything against setting down roots?"

His gaze pinned her. "You mean marrying?"

"No," she said, somewhat angry. "I didn't mean marrying. But it seems to me you'd make my choice in a flash. You seem to equate staying in one place with stagnation. Don't you ever envision giving up your rolling-stone lifestyle?"

"There are several tribes that have been nomads for centuries. And have prospered."

"You're talking about tribes like the Masai in Africa and the nomads of Asia, who herd cattle and other livestock out of economic necessity. You don't have to build up a new camp every few days to survive. You could have a regular job and get paid quite handsomely, I'm sure."

His expression became unreadable. "You sound like my father. He's been trying to get me in the family business since college. But I'd rather make it on my own than through the offices of Wayne Sheridan, one half of Brown and Sheridan Engineering, Inc."

She was alert to the bitterness in his tone. "Do you think it's wrong of your father to want you to follow in his footsteps?"

He shifted and lay on his back. "I'm not my father. I like my job, I like traveling, I like pitting myself against the elements. He wants to dress me in three piece suits and sit me down in a conference room to give orders to people who probably know a hundred times more than I do. No, thanks. I'd rather be fighting an encroaching jungle or a desert storm. There's a lot of satisfaction in knowing you've battled great odds and come out ahead."

"I imagine your father thought he'd like to have all that ability and drive on his side. He must have a lot of battles to fight himself—deadlines, lowering production, strikes, incompetent workers, lack of necessary materials . . ."

"My father would fall instantly in love with you," Burke said dryly.

She smiled at him and said softly, "I just don't think you've really thought it out. And who knows, if you'd let yourself try, you might even like working in your father's company."

"Are you acquainted with my father? Did he send you here to soften me up?"

She laughed at the incipient suspicion in his voice. *"You're* the one who kidnaped *me,* remember? Besides, I don't get involved in family quarrels. An outsider always gets caught in the middle."

"Not in this case," he said. "I think you and Wayne have a lot in common."

"Are you an only child?"

"No. I have two younger brothers, Lee and Darryll. Lee's the middle one, and he's a high school principal. He's married to a nurse, Alice. They have triplets, Emily, Scott, and Wayne. Initially, Alice had trouble conceiving, but the fertility drug she took worked like a charm." His voice grew soft as he said, "The triplets are now in their terrible twos, and they give their parents more than enough to do."

His expression relaxed as he talked of the triplets, and his gaze was far-seeing, lost in remembrance. Dale gave him some quiet time, studying him, surprised at yet another facet of the man. He obviously adored his niece and nephews.

"Will you be seeing them soon?" she asked finally.

"The triplets? At Thanksgiving. A family tradition. All the Sheridans get together then, and my father helps my mother cook for the whole clan."

"What does your mother do?"

"She's a lawyer. Dad tried to draft her into the company, too, but she's too smart. She knew they'd be at each other like cats and dogs. She's a partner in a big law firm in New Jersey."

"Is that where you're from?"

He nodded. "Elizabeth, New Jersey. I used to keep a town house in the Midwest, where my company is based. But I'm not home too often, so I'm renting it out. During my vacations I either come here and go houseboating or go to my parents for the holidays."

Dale began to feel the chill of the night air and snuggled deeper under the soft, warm cover. As Burke had predicted, the rain had begun to decrease in intensity and now beat softly, erratically, on their cloth roof, dripping over the sides in little rivulets. She breathed in deeply of the rain-fresh air.

"What about your other brother?"

"Darryll? He's studying ballet, and my father has finally learned to take that in stride. Darryll is very quiet and reserved, but he's got a core of solid steel. When Dad saw he couldn't dissuade Darryll from his chosen profession, he eased off."

"Has he eased off you, too?"

Burke rested his head on his bent arm and studied her. "Perceptive, aren't you? Yes, he's let up some. But he still gets in his yearly sermon at Thanksgiving."

"Smart man, your father."

"Why do I get the feeling you're on his side?" Burke asked wryly.

"Maybe because I can imagine how it must feel for your father to work hard for something and then have no one to carry on his efforts."

"Are you saying I should put aside my own interests in favor of my father's?" Burke asked in a dangerously quiet voice.

Dale sighed. "Listen, it's none of my business—"

"That hasn't stopped you so far."

"All right. No, I don't think you should put aside your personal interests and just do whatever your dad asks. But since he's got an engineering firm, and you're an engineer, it seems to me there should be some way for you to meet each other halfway."

"In my father's book, meeting him halfway means doing things his way. I've got my own life to lead."

Dale decided to drop the subject. Burke was stubborn, and apparently his father was, too. She suspected the greatest stumbling block between them was pride, but it really wasn't her concern.

She shifted to her back as Burke had, and studied the mobile shapes the dying firelight cast on the canvas high above her head. She heard movement on her side and turned her head in time to see Burke get out of his sleeping bag and walk to the fire. He added more twigs to it, and some cones, which instantly permeated the air with a sharp, pine scent.

Getting down on his haunches, his wiry muscles rippling in back and thighs, he rearranged the almost spent logs in the fire, adding a few new ones. "Do you want to go back to the houseboat, or do you prefer spending the rest of the night here?" he asked.

Dale took a look at her watch and saw that it was

already after three. "I'm nice and warm, and the air smells wonderful. I'd rather stay here."

"Okay." He went back to his sleeping bag and got in without looking at her. Turning his back on her, he said, "Good night."

Somewhat hurt at his abruptness, Dale didn't answer. Obviously, Burke was angry about something. And that could only be her opinion on his joining his father's firm. Burke was an adventurer. He liked to take chances, live dangerously, test himself against different climates, circumstances, environments. But it also took guts to stick it out in one place, to fight for one's dream. Staying in one place required its own brand of courage.

She hadn't been thinking of marriage when she'd asked Burke if he'd thought about settling down, but his attitude reminded her of Joel's. Her former fiancé had also been wary of commitment, of settling down. She'd been very convenient to have around, Dale had realized after almost three years of loving Joel. She'd always been there for him; yet, he had never been there for her. And no relationship could survive when all the giving was on one side.

Her voice quite cool, she echoed Burke's "Good night" before turning on her side so her back was to him. She dropped off to sleep with the scent of rain-washed air in her nostrils, and the image of a bronzed, impossible man on her retinas.

- 6 -

NORMALLY NOT A morning person, Dale had no trouble waking up with an incentive like the appetizing aroma of eggs and bacon and freshly brewed coffee.

She opened her eyes to find Burke grinning at her from the campfire, where he was preparing breakfast. "I've been making enough noise to wake up the proverbial dead for the past hour, but I see that the only way to reach you *is* through your stomach," he said.

She stretched sinuously, seeing his gaze lower with pleasing predictability to her bust, which was accentuated by her arching motion and the loving cling of her soft wool sweater.

"What can I say? My appetite is always ravenous in the fresh air."

He opened his mouth to say something—no doubt a reference to other appetites—but with commendable restraint closed it again. He motioned to yet another

73

log he'd found in the forest behind him, and said, "Have a seat. The chef will serve you."

The scrambled eggs and bacon were the best breakfast she'd ever had. Dale savored the hot, delicious food, and didn't refuse seconds. Burke's eyes went instinctively to her flat stomach and full but trim thighs, and he said, "I'm not sure where you put all that."

"Unfortunately, I can't claim a speedy metabolism," she said, smiling.

"How do you keep that gorgeous figure, then?" he asked as he refilled first her cup, then his, with more coffee.

"I put in long hours at work," she replied as she put the last exquisite bite of scrambled egg in her mouth. "And I walk every day. It helps clear the cobwebs, and I get a lot of my thinking done that way, away from phones and constant interruptions."

Returning his appreciative look, she allowed her gaze to rove over his jean-and-knit-shirt–clad body, and asked, "How about you? Do you exercise regularly?"

"Every day, but not at health clubs. On my job, you pinch-hit whenever and wherever you're needed. The deserts and jungles of this world often cut into your manpower, disabling people or exposing them to diseases like malaria and dysentery. I've made my way through jungles with a machete, helped with the actual construction of bridges and buildings, and even found my way through a desert storm once when the natives refused to work."

"And you can put up with such a sedate vacation as this one? I'd have said yachts and yawls are more your style," she couldn't resist saying.

A look of irritation crossed his features. "I don't

value speed for speed's sake, any more than I seek excitement purely for cheap thrills. I like a challenge and the intrinsic satisfaction one finds in a hard, demanding job well done."

"And those hard, demanding jobs can only be found outside the States?"

He paused in the act of cleaning the frying pan with some sand he'd brought up from the beach.

"Does my job bother you? Or the fact that I'm not afraid to go after what I want?" he challenged.

That certainly was laying it on the line. And in a way, he was right. Had it not been for her experience with Joel, she would not be keeping Burke at arm's length. But she'd been deeply hurt by her former fiancé. The past—and its salutary lessons—was not erased that quickly.

"Shouldn't we get going?" she inquired lightly. "I seem to have slept part of the morning away. I don't want to miss anything of my short vacation."

Burke looked at her silently but didn't press his question. Together they made short order of cleaning up, leaving the beautiful spot as clean and unspoiled as they'd found it.

The rest of the morning passed in a pleasing blur. Burke had her take the wheel of the *Seaprincess* and explained more about possible dangers to be faced while boating on the Mississippi. The river was once more smooth and tranquil, the angry waters of last night a thing of the past. The sky was a limpid, eye-hurting blue in which not even a fleecy cloud was visible.

Toward noon the storm-induced coolness had disappeared and they took turns changing, Burke into shorts and a tank top of fine mesh, Dale into red shorts and a white and red striped top with capped sleeves and an elasticized hem that circled her midriff.

They decided to skip lunch in favor of reaching a cove Burke had made sound too attractive to pass up. It meant a slight detour, but he had assured Dale it was worth it. The perfect weather and magnificent scenery had mellowed both their tempers, although the underlying tension was still between them, temporarily dormant.

Shortly after three o'clock, Burke announced, "There it is."

Dale, who had been piloting for the past hour, leaned forward eagerly.

"Where?"

"To the left. You're going to have to enter that small river that empties onto the Mississippi."

"Do you know how the Mississippi came by its name?" Dale asked as she guided the houseboat into the tributary.

Burke leaned forward, his lean hip touching hers as he looked straight ahead. "From the days of the explorer Père Marquette to the mythical Tom Sawyer, it's acquired many names. But the one derived from the Ojibway name *Mississippi* has endured."

"And it means?"

"Great River. The first time I ever boated on the Mississippi was while I was still in college. A professor of mine, part Indian, asked me to go with him, and told me about all the kinds of legends and folklore associated with Old Man River."

Dale took her eye off the river for a minute to ask him to recount some of those legends, when Burke jumped forward and grabbed the wheel.

"Watch out! There are some tricky, submerged rocks around here. This portion of the stream is somewhat treacherous."

With his direction, Dale navigated the *Seaprincess* into the cove. As she turned off the motor and let her muscles go limp, she saw that the spot was everything Burke had described and more.

The sand gleamed white-gold in the radiant sunlight, and the cliffs ranged from white to an ochre-red in the distance. The foliage was a brilliant green and wild flowers abounded, coexisting in aesthetic seas of pink, yellow, and lilac.

"Want to have a picnic?" Burke asked, his eyes taking in her pleasure with an unfathomable, calculating glance.

"You've made me an offer I can't refuse," Dale said, laughing, her earlier displeasure of the morning forgotten as she responded with a teasing, lighthearted tone.

Burke smiled, but his attitude was guarded. If she hadn't felt she knew him better than that, Dale would have said he was playing hard to get.

Which was ridiculous. Whatever else Burke was, he was not conniving. At least, she didn't want to credit him with deceit. Deciding he must be thinking about work or other problems, Dale pushed her suspicions away. She was determined to enjoy the beautiful day and the breathtaking surroundings.

An hour later, Dale and Burke lay in the sun, she on the white blanket they'd brought along, he on the grass. Although the sun had begun its ritual of descent, its rays were still potent and Burke had taken off his tank top. Looking at the muscles that ridged his chest and arms, Dale decided she envied the sweet, fresh grass that surrounded him.

Feeling a strange restlessness grip her, she sat up.
The elastic below her breasts felt binding in the intense
heat, and she juggled it about, trying to relieve the
prickling the material imposed. Another sort of prickling invaded her pores, and her head snapped up to
encounter Burke's smoldering glance on her.

She stopped breathing as he got up and slowly
approached to sit down next to her, his long legs
stretched out in front of him in the opposite direction
so that he could face her. A sensual paralysis gripped
her. She'd been aware of Burke to a degree she'd
never been with any other man, including Joel. The
restlessness that had made her nerves stand at attention
was induced by him and him alone, and Dale found
herself ill-equipped to handle the intensity of her response.

His gaze traveled her face slowly, dropping to her
neck and ascending again, concentrating on lips that
responded to his visual caress as if to his touch. As
his eyes met hers, his hands lifted to her hair and
untied the red ribbon that secured her thick braid.

He combed his fingers through her hair, pulling
the long black tresses forward until they fell in gleaming twin masses over and past her shoulders, forming
a dramatic contrast to her light top and creamy skin.
His eyes sent her hot, intimate messages, even as his
hands continued their seductive rhythm in her hair,
rubbing the silky strands between his fingertips and
against her own skin.

"You should wear your hair down more often," he
told her in a muffled tone as he buried his face in the
fragrant, silken mass.

She'd been told that before, but the suggestion had

never held the import it did now. She remained motionless, knowing that at this moment her defenses were at their weakest. She might have enough willpower not to seek him out, but in this heated instant, she didn't think she could resist any advances on his part.

He continued caressing her hair, stroking it against his face and inhaling deeply of its rich, violet scent. Then he went oddly still for a second before straightening and leaping to his feet in a catlike motion.

Dale looked up at him uncomprehendingly, her black hair streaming about her flushed face and heaving chest. Burke had not touched anything besides her hair, had done no more than look at her with hungry, possessing eyes. Yet, that hunger had been instantly transmitted to her, and she'd wanted to be possessed and in turn possess with a voracity that matched his own.

He looked down at her with unreadable eyes, his own uncertain breathing the only indication he was in any way affected.

"I'm going to do a bit of exploring," he announced, and turned, leaving her to look after him with troubled, confused eyes.

Burke returned three hours later, boarding the *Seaprincess* just as the red sun sank in the horizon, leaving the sky a smudged canvas with purple, orange, and cerise streaks.

His black mood had apparently dissipated, but Dale knew that they were only burying their emotions. Those feelings were bound to burst through at any unguarded moment, but neither of them seemed inclined to take the easy way out and avoid a confrontation. Neither she nor Burke was prepared to leave the *Seaprincess;* that had been decided the day she had tried to leave Burke behind and he had caught up with her, containing his obvious rage and proving surprisingly understanding.

Dale wasn't sure exactly why neither of them was willing to depart. It could be that both of them had a generous share of pride. Or both were curious to see what would happen. Or they were both too attracted to each other to let go until something was resolved.

Certainly, running away never solved anything, Dale reflected as Burke walked past her to take a shower. She was living proof of that. She'd come aboard the *Seaprincess* to decide about the move to St. Louis, but she hadn't yet resolved the issue. Moreover, now she had an additional problem, one that was proving even harder to solve.

As she began fixing a mushroom omelet she told herself that work problems might be difficult to handle, but affairs of the heart were impossible.

Affairs of the heart! Dale stood stock-still, with the pan in one hand and the mushrooms in the other. Since when had she begun thinking of Burke in terms of an affair, and worse, an affair of the heart?

The sound of Burke's off-key singing drifted out to her, and Dale quickly began mixing the ingredients, adding some tomatoes and onions as well as numerous spices. A mouth-watering aroma was emanating from the golden-brown omelet when a pair of large hands circled her waist from behind.

She jumped, burning herself in the process, and uttered a loud curse.

"Temper, temper," Burke said, swiftly turning off

the burner, grabbing her wrist, and pulling her to the sink.

"Let's see," he murmured, inspecting the tender, red area on her hand before letting it soak under the cold water. "You'll live."

"Thanks for the vote of confidence," she said smartly, inhaling his woodsy, clean male aroma and trying to decide which had the more appetizing fragrance, Burke or the omelet.

As if on cue, her stomach grumbled and Burke turned off the faucet. He lifted her hand to his lips and dropped little kisses on it. "There. Does it feel all better now?"

"It would feel better if you hadn't sneaked up on me," she told him crossly, thinking that an attack on so many fronts, on so many senses at once, was definitely not fair play. "Shall we eat before the omelet gets cold?"

"Amen," Burke said, his eyes twinkling. Apparently, his good humor was completely restored.

"Mushrooms," he exclaimed as he motioned her to sit down and began serving. "How did you know I liked them?"

"The refrigerator's half full with them," she told him wryly. "It didn't take Sherlock Holmes to figure that one out."

His compliments were effusive, and he devoured his portion of the omelet and part of hers in short order. "Are you sure you don't mind giving this up? It's a culinary treat."

"I'm fine," she soothed his guilt as he put the last bite in his mouth. "I love fresh vegetables; I was munching away on carrots, celery sticks, and green pepper while you were gone."

There was a gentle rebuke in her voice, and he looked up, guilt written all over his bronzed features again.

"I'm sorry I left so abruptly, but I had a lot of thinking to do," he told her.

"And did you get everything sorted out?"

His gaze was honest. "No. But I was in danger of breaking my promise to you. And I don't want you to think that I tried to talk you into staying just to acquire a convenient sleeping partner."

Her gaze softened and she told him, "I never thought that. You're attractive enough to have someone with you on board, and you did tell me you wanted solitude. I appreciate the fact that you didn't throw me overboard."

He shrugged. "How could I get rid of you, when the mix-up wasn't your fault? But I meant what I said: I won't come on too heavy . . . or at least I'll try not to."

She returned his steady gaze and smiled.

"Fair enough." Gathering their plates, she said, "How about some games?"

"Spin the bottle?" he asked hopefully.

"I'm sure if anyone knows all the adult variations, it's you. But no, I was thinking more in terms of backgammon, or checkers, or UNO. I found several games when I was going through the cupboards for food."

"We can start with checkers," Burke said as he got up to help her clear the table and dry the dishes. As they were putting everything away, she asked him, "Were you planning on feeding an army while on

vacation? I couldn't believe the amount of fresh and
canned food I found."

He began setting up the checkers game and grinned.
"I don't get to eat many of my favorite foods in the
places I work at. Even plain hamburgers become a
luxury, let alone steaks or mushrooms."

"I made some apple pie. Would you like some with
coffee later?"

"Later? Why wait? Right now!"

He went in search of and discovered the fresh-
baked pie on a windowsill, and ordered her to sit down
while he prepared the coffee.

Dale smiled as she saw him sneak a bit of the crust
and reflected that this was the Burke she liked best—
the uninhibited, free, fun-loving man she'd met just
a few short days ago. She knew the *Seaprincess* and
the real world were two different matters, but for now,
she intended to enjoy this interlude and Burke's company to the fullest.

"Okay, pay up. I want my prize now."

Dale looked at Burke suspiciously. They'd been
playing for almost four hours and had changed from
checkers to backgammon at his insistence. She weighed
the dice in her hands as if to check their trustworthi-
ness. "Are you sure these aren't loaded?"

He grinned. "I wouldn't know. Wyatt's the one
who provides the games. You'd have to ask him."

"I think I'd like a rematch in checkers. I was beating the pants off you until you decided you were
getting bored and insisted we switch games."

Burke stretched like a supremely fit feline, his dark
blue knit shirt stretching lovingly over the marvelous

torso. "That's not exactly correct. You vetoed our playing poker—"

"Your version was predictably strip poker."

"—and you didn't beat the pants off me. You just won a couple of games—"

"Ten to your two..."

"—and now you're proving you're a sore loser because I creamed you in backgammon."

Dale leaned back, hooking her elbows on the back of the chair, conscious that her breasts jutted out enticingly under the embroidered eyelet blouse.

"How come you didn't think of playing for prizes when I was creaming *you?*"

"I did. I wanted to play strip poker, remember? That would have proved sufficient reward to me. I didn't have much to lose, if my memory serves me correctly. You've already seen everything there is to see of me."

"Odious man! To bring that up now in the middle of this argument."

"Well, you do have me at a disadvantage. I'm an open book to you. Care to make it even?"

She snorted. "My seeing you in the buff was pure accident."

"I wonder. . . . You were just dying to see whether the body matched the magnificent voice."

He leaned forward, an irrepressible glint in his eyes, and Dale couldn't help smiling. She wiped the grin off her face quickly, but not before Burke saw it.

"I saw that. Admit it! That morning was one of the high points of your life."

"Don't you wish," she said scoffingly, privately agreeing that she'd never seen a more beautiful male body than his. "But it certainly seemed to be quite high for you, you conceited..."

Her words strangled in her throat at the look that came over his features. She realized what she'd said and turned beet red.

Intending only to escape the ribbing that she knew he'd subject her to after her unguarded, provoking statement, she shot up and attempted to pass by him. But Burke was in the direct route to the bedrooms, and he hooked one of his legs with hers, tripping her. Dale yelped at the prospect of sprawling on her face on the carpet, but Burke grabbed her just in time, breaking her fall.

He let himself drop, maneuvering her body on top of his, and then rolled her over, pinning her underneath him. "Can't take the heat, can you?" he taunted.

Her face turned even redder at his words, and when he accommodated his body comfortably on top of hers, the added heat made her feel on the verge of apoplexy.

"If there's one thing I hate, it's a man using his superior strength to subdue a woman," she told him loftily.

"Oh, but I'm not using force," he said innocently. "Look, Ma, no hands." He braced both arms on either side of her. "I merely saved you from a nasty fall and happened to accompany you on the way down."

"In that case, I'm grateful for your assistance, but now I'd like to get up."

"As soon as you tell me you'll deliver what I won."

"A massage?" she scoffed. "I'm not an expert. I'm sure if you go to a professional masseuse you'll get a better deal all around."

He picked up one of her hands, which were pushing

against his shoulders, and stroked it. "But I want *these* hands. They're special, just like those tropical-green eyes, and that black hair you've tortured on top of your head." He lifted his upper torso and looked at her bust. "And just like those perfect breasts of yours, with those cherry-red nipples that are so luscious peeping through this thin yellow material—"

"All right, all right," she interjected hastily. "You win. I'll give you your damn massage."

He grinned, a grin she'd seen duplicated in a shark on one of those *National Geographic* specials.

"I knew you'd see it my way," he told her, getting up and offering her his hand.

She disdained it, giving him an affronted look, and asked, "Where do you want it?" His eyes glinted and she added swiftly, "The massage. Where do you want me to give you your massage?"

He indicated the couch in one corner. "That'll be fine."

With the unselfconscious grace that characterized his actions, Burke pulled off his top and lay down on the striped gold and black couch.

Dale looked longingly at his smooth, tanned back, and found her hands itching to touch the gleaming bronze skin. She hadn't been opposed to playing for stakes, but knowing how good she was at backgammon, she'd never dreamed she'd lose.

And now she was faced with the unnerving prospect of giving Burke a massage, when it was taking all her willpower to act cool and collected around him.

When she didn't move, Burke lifted his head and pinned her with his blue-green gaze. "Trying to sneak out of it? There aren't too many places to hide on this houseboat, large and comfortable as it is."

"I always said this boat wasn't big enough for the two of us," she muttered as she went to sit next to him and ungraciously plopped her hands on his back.

She began tentatively, rolling the flesh under her hands and kneading, feeling the pleasure darts that traveled from her brain to the rest of her body.

So concerned was she with corralling her galloping yearning that her massage was less than satisfactory. She felt Burke wriggle underneath her hands until finally he exploded.

"Dammit, woman, I won't melt! Will you give me a proper massage?"

"I told you I'm not a qualified masseuse. But if you want me to work you over harder than this, I'll be happy to oblige."

And she did.

Getting on her knees, she rearranged his body so she could put one leg on either side of him. Burke sighed with pleasure as he felt the warm skin of her inner thighs. Fixing the hem of her brief yellow shorts, which rode up between her thighs in the position she was in, she made herself comfortable and mentally rolled up her sleeves.

The first blow caught him in the middle of his back. Burke yelped, riding up off the couch in surprise. But Dale pressed her weight against his lower back and made him lie down again. Using the heels of her hands, she began a quick chopping motion upward and downward, increasing in pressure and tempo as she got into the swing of things.

Burke's groans reverberated against her legs, and she began attacking his muscles, rolling his flesh between her long, slender fingers as if it were bread dough. Burke's groans became muffled sounds of pleasure as he settled even deeper into the couch and put his head on his folded hands.

Dale could feel the flesh of her thighs burn where they came in contact with his, and she was acutely and pleasurably aware of the firm buttocks under her derriere. To distract herself from her wayward thoughts, and to waylay her body from its strong longings, she switched her approach again, beginning the karate chops once more.

This time her movements were more practiced, and she was able to put more strength into her thumping. The groans started again and increased in volume in proportion to the strength of her blows. Dale smiled with satisfaction and asked sweetly, "Anything wrong, Burke?"

His answer was a low, strangled, "No, no. Nothing's wrong. Everything's just peachy."

"Would you like me to quit? You know I don't have much experience at this . . ."

He raised his head to speak, each word punctuated by a blow. "No—just—continue—you're—doing—fine . . ."

"If you're sure . . ."

"Quite—sure."

Dale decided he'd had enough and got in a few more punches before switching to some hard stroking. Sliding her hands upward along his back, she worked on his neck muscles, feeling the cords of tension dissolve under her kneading. Unwilling to deny herself the pleasure, she buried her hands in his thick blond hair and began to rub his scalp, her legs also rubbing along his sides with every rhythmic motion she made.

The mortal groans changed to grunts of pleasure as Dale continued her ministrations to Burke's head and neck and shoulders. The feel of his hair, flesh, and muscles was heavenly, and she smiled as she remembered being jealous of the grass that afternoon.

So lost was she in her own pleasure that she didn't at first notice how even his breathing had become until she realized that the broad chest was practically motionless. She stopped working and stared down at him. Burke neither protested nor moved. Dale jumped up and down experimentally, riding him like a pony, but he still didn't move.

The infuriating man was fast asleep!

- 7 -

"YOU SURE YOU don't want to come along?" Burke asked the next morning as she lay sunning on the top deck.

Dale raised her head from the lounger to tell him lazily, "Positive. You may have gotten your beauty sleep last night from my wonderful massage, but I didn't have anyone to return the favor. I'd rather rest than fish."

"I wouldn't exactly call it a wonderful massage," Burke said wryly.

"It did the trick," she replied sleeplily.

"That's because you beat me senseless," he told her, picking up the lotion and putting it within reach of her hand.

She laughed weakly. "Good luck with your fishing," she drawled.

"Thanks," Burke said. "Hope you're agreeable to having fish for dinner."

"Great. You can clean and cook it," she said before laying her head down again and surrendering her mind and body to the beautiful dry heat of the morning.

"Just don't overdo the sunbathing," Burke warned before he left her. "I don't want to find *you* cooked when I return."

"I'll be careful," Dale murmured, fast asleep before Burke had even left the *Seaprincess*.

She awoke an hour later and decided to take a shower before putting on some more lotion and resuming her position in the deck. She searched the shore to see if she could spot Burke, but he was nowhere to be seen. Enjoying the temporary solitude, Dale decided to do something she didn't usually get the chance to try: nude sunbathing. Running downstairs to get a wrap, she took off her bikini and lay on her back, smothering herself with a sunscreen.

Every little noise she heard made her jump. She was obviously not used to this, and despite feeling comfortable and satisfied about her body, Dale reflected that she'd never be a centerfold. She remembered Burke's nonchalance and thought that he certainly had the type of body to grace *Playgirl,* probably would even be able to carry it off with finesse. He was neither shy nor inhibited.

After checking every few minutes to see if Burke was coming, she decided he was probably like every typical fisherman and wouldn't be returning for a few hours yet, so she might as well relax and enjoy herself. With this decision, she smeared some more lotion on and rolled over on to her stomach.

A very pleasant dream made Dale smile and shift her body into a more comfortable position on the lounger. Something very cool was being applied to her back, and the feeling was exquisite. She moaned with pleasure, arching her back against the liquid and the wonderful stroking, which seemed to reach to the very center of her and relax every muscle.

Slowly, consciousness returned and Dale opened her eyes, seeing the deck turned to a shimmering white under the hot rays of the sun. Gradually, she became aware that the wonderful stroking was being done by hands with great expertise. She attempted to sit up, but Burke soothed her back down, continuing his massage with palms, fingers, and elbows.

Finally, Dale couldn't take any more, and she grabbed at her terry-cloth wrap, holding it in front of her as she turned around on the lounger.

"Fish not biting?" she asked thickly, her tongue and brain not functioning quite properly yet.

"They were very cooperative, but I've told you before how I feel about warm-blooded mammals."

"Does that mean we have fried fish for dinner tonight?"

"As well as fresh salad and strawberry Jell-O."

"Sounds marvelous," she said, realizing she'd skipped lunch.

Apparently, he realized the same thing, because he said, "I think that's enough sun for one day. You've turned quite pink, and I don't think you want to add sunburn to your memories from this vacation."

"You think right," she said, feeling marvelously rested and content. She looked up at him, amazed that she didn't feel self-conscious about lying there with only a scanty wrap covering her intimate parts. On the contrary, everything felt absolutely right.

Which was the more reason for her to get below.

"Do you mind moving so I can put this on and go below?"

He sighed. "I don't suppose you'll let me help you on with the wrap?"

She laughed, completely awake now and very aware of his magnetic presence.

"I think I can manage by myself."

"Well, if you need any assistance..."

"I'll know where not to look," she told him, returning his wide grin.

He smoothed his hand along her exposed flanks and got up reluctantly. Bending, he traced the straight ridge of her nose with his forefinger and dropped a kiss on the slightly upturned tip.

"Don't take too long."

She smiled. "I won't."

Dale took a longer shower this time and lathered her skin gingerly. She'd overdone the sunbathing a bit, but luckily she didn't burn easily. Her skin was most tender in those places that didn't normally see the sun, but after putting on some lotion, she didn't feel much discomfort.

She found herself strangely reluctant to rejoin Burke. His gentle gesture had wrenched her heart, and she'd realized then that there was more to what she felt for him than physical attraction. That was strong, yes. But it wouldn't be so powerful if she did not also admire his strength of character, his integrity, and his magnetic presence. It was his intelligence and wit that differentiated him from other men she'd known. She'd been careful earlier because she'd felt vulnerable. She hadn't wanted to be carried away by passion.

But she'd had ample time to think things over while

showering and getting dressed. As she braided her hair and piled it on top of her head in a thick coronet, she knew that what she'd feared had come to pass: She'd fallen in love with Burke.

From the beginning, she'd known what an emotional threat he'd be. She'd recognized that he was an even bigger threat than Joel, and had tried to avoid a confrontation by leaving him behind. Her desire for solitude had only been part of her motivation; she'd also been afraid of what his continued presence might mean.

And her fears had proved justified. Only she was no longer afraid.

As she applied some violet scent on her pulse points, then smoothed the folds of her embroidered white-on-black caftan, Dale came to a decision. She'd never been in favor of running away; she'd broken up with Joel only when she'd realized that nothing permanent would come of their relationship. But Burke had a more complex personality than Joel: She was willing to gamble that he had a lot to give. And she wanted to give to him.

She left her bedroom and went toward the kitchen, her heart pounding joyously. She knew Burke wouldn't make the first move, but she was prepared to come to him as he had predicted she would. Now that she'd faced up to the fact that she was in love with him, she could do nothing else. Still, Dale knew she was taking a risk. Although Burke had shown her tenderness, playfulness, and caring, she didn't know if he was in love with her.

But she was willing to find out...

The evening was cool and clear, with millions of stars peeping from the dark, velvety firmament. The fat sphere of the moon diffused its silver light over the river and the *Seaprincess,* casting a magical mother-of-pearl translucence over everything it touched.

The nocturnal breeze carried aboard the fresh scent of grass and flowers from shore as Dale and Burke sipped from their cocktails on top of the deck. Dale's dramatic caftan spilled over the yellow lounger where she reclined, and its midnight folds—except for the white embroidery on the mandarin collar and full, flowing sleeves—were lost in the darkness of the night.

"It's so beautifully peaceful, isn't it?" Burke's voice floated quietly to her from the opposite side of the sun deck.

"Yes. I can see why you come here every year. It must be a sort of renewal for you."

"Exactly. That's why I keep coming back, why I'll continue to do so. The river has its own ancient, timeless magic. Just hearing its soft, whispering sound somehow makes me glad to be alive, away from all deadlines and pressures. It reaffirms my existence."

Dale savored his words. Burke might not know it, but he was a romantic at heart. He was something of a loner, too, as she was, enjoying his own company. But his appreciation of nature's beauty and its restorative power touched a deep, responsive chord in her.

"I'm glad you caught up with me when I tried to ditch you," she told him.

His silence told her that her statement surprised him.

Finally, he replied, "Well, I have to admit I rather stacked the odds in my favor. I picked that lonely, insipid stretch of land because I could anchor fairly close to shore and could monitor what you were doing. I was fairly convinced that you were going to try to give me the slip."

"So you weren't asleep at all." It was more a statement than a question.

"I was rather enjoying your exaggerated casualness," he said, chuckling.

She remembered back on her seemingly foolproof plan, the care she'd taken, when all the while Burke had been keeping an eye on *her*. But it didn't seem to matter anymore.

"How were you able to catch up with me?" she asked, feeling free to discuss things now and wanting everything in the open.

"I was on both my high school and college swim teams. So you see, you really never stood a chance."

She recalled that moment as if it were happening now. It would always remain vivid in her memory. And how different things would be if she'd succeeded.

"Want another drink before I get dinner started?" Burke asked.

She sipped the last of her Bacardi on the rocks and put the glass on the deck. Taking a deep breath, she said softly, "No, I don't want another drink. And I'd rather wait on dinner."

She knew she'd surprised him again. They'd usually eaten dinner by now, but she had asked Burke if he'd mind waiting tonight, since she wanted to relax on top of the deck for a while.

She was glad darkness blanketed them when she spoke. "I want you to make love to me."

The silence was tangible. Dale thought that perhaps Burke had not heard her, and she licked her dry lips, prepared to repeat her request.

But it wasn't necessary. She heard Burke set down his own drink and then walk across to her side.

She moved slightly to allow him to sit next to her.

"Are you sure?" he asked seriously.

She was grateful he did not make her repeat her words or pretend to misunderstand. Although she was in love with him, she had only realized it tonight. The feelings were fresh—and very scary. She wanted to take her chance with him, because she knew she'd regret it all her life if she didn't. But she didn't want Burke to have even an inkling of how deep her emotions ran. She wanted tonight to be special but natural. She didn't want him to feel coerced or under obligation in any way.

"Quite sure. As you predicted, I did break down and ask you. Your record should now be perfect."

His hand lifted to protest her flippant remark, and his fingers brushed tenderly over her lips, then rested there. "Don't. If I hadn't given you my word, I'd have asked you. But I didn't want you to think—"

"That I had to work off my passage," she finished for him, teasingly.

She felt a warm swell of tenderness at his effort to set her at ease. From many other men, she'd have expected some triumphant crowing. But Burke was not like other men. She'd sensed a quiet strength in him, and a concurrent sensitivity and tenderness. She hadn't been wrong in her assessment.

The hand on her lips lowered to her throat, and Burke let his fingers rest on her life pulse. It began racing under his touch, heating her blood.

"What's the answer to my proposition? Yes or no?" she asked huskily, feeling oddly serene.

"Lady, how can you even doubt it? It's been hell trying to act the perfect gentleman around you, Dale," he told her, curving one hand around her waist and drawing her to a sitting position.

"I don't think you've been a *perfect* gentleman," she said softly, letting her eyes rove lovingly over his features, which were bathed in moonlight. "But I did appreciate the effort."

He chuckled, and his other arm went beneath her thighs. Sudden clouds cut off the moonbeams, and everything was dusky as he picked her up and placed her on the deck.

The coolness of the deck was welcome in the sudden heat of night. Dale lifted her arm to Burke's short-sleeved white shirt, feeling her way to the buttons. As she began opening them Burke's hands went to her hair and started unpinning it, letting the soft mass fall about her face and shoulders.

The clouds that had been teasing the moon moved aside temporarily, and a misty gleam silvered Burke's glistening torso and turned his hair into white gold. His arms reached for her again as he leaned over her, and with excruciating slowness he began to unzip the caftan. Dale hadn't worn a bra underneath its loose comfort, and as he eased the satiny garment open, his knuckles rubbed against the silken swell of her breast. She gasped, the sudden sensation unexpected in its intensity, and her eyes lowered from the top of his bent head to study his long, powerful fingers. The silken fuzz covering their gentle strength now gleamed golden in the moonlight and contrasted starkly with her paler skin.

His fingers continued their slow, easy task until the caftan was unzipped to her navel. He pushed the material aside and bent down to place a kiss on her stomach, the feminine muscles contracting under the light, sensual glide of his lips.

He raised his golden head, his eyes now a midnight blue, burning with a contained, smoldering desire that somehow seemed more powerful, more elemental, than any wild grasping and groping.

His self-control scared Dale on more than one level, because it showed her so conclusively what a tight rein Burke had over his emotions. He had desired her from the first time they'd laid eyes on each other, but he hadn't forced himself on her in any way. He'd fulfilled his promise to let her make the first move, and the alacrity with which he'd accepted her overture indicated the level of his need.

As his hands traveled upward from her hips to her shoulders with maddening slowness, savoring en route the soft feel of the fabric covering her rapidly swelling breasts, a tremor of half-anticipation, half-fear, rippled through her.

There was so little time left for both of them, and yet, if she hadn't made her move tonight, she would never have known the bittersweet reality of Burke's possession...

The black caftan began to slide from her shoulders, the rich material descending teasingly on her sensitized skin, prickling her flesh, which was already covered with goosebumps from the coolness of the nocturnal river breeze and the feather-light touch of Burke's callused fingers.

The material ballooned and settled around her waist as Dale pulled her arms out, and Burke got up with one lithe motion, removing his white slacks and tossing them in a dark corner of the boat. Dale's eyes shone with love and desire, their night-emerald brightness traveling over the wide expanse of his shoulders and chest. His muscles moved fluidly under the tight, glistening skin as he pivoted toward her once more. Her gaze descended with a feeling of déjà vu as she took in his narrow waist and slender hips, which tapered into long, perfectly proportioned legs.

As Burke knelt before her, his desire proudly obvious in the whipcord-lean physique, her whole being seemed to yearn for him. Burke's eyes never left her face, but he seemed to sense the involuntary reaction of her body, because his hands homed in instinctively on her engorged breasts, his rough palms cupping their creamy smoothness and pressing against the hardened tips, which strained to meet his touch.

His name escaped her lips in a whimper of need, and she repeated it in a vow of love. Burke's hands slid down her body, pulling the rest of her dress down, and Dale sought the support of his arms as her world became a dizzying spiral of sensation. She got to her knees so he could slip the caftan past her hips, and then his hands were grazing her skin, scorching the rounded curve of hip and thigh as he pushed down her lace bikini panties. Then, with a quick, smooth movement, he disposed of caftan and panties in the same general direction his slacks had landed.

Burke arched her body to his so that her torso was curved away from him, but their lower bodies met with scalding, breath-taking intimacy. Dale gasped as she felt his pulsing maleness seek entry between her quivering thighs, and her legs parted willingly to accommodate the satisfying contact.

A groan was torn from deep within Burke's body as his hardness found warm refuge in her softness, and he murmured huskily, "You're lovely, Dale. A marvel of smooth, creamy skin and glorious curves."

Dale reveled in his words, giddy with the excitement of pleasing him, dazed with the overpowering effect he had on the senses he was playing upon with the leisure and expertise of a virtuoso.

His hands grasped her hips to pull her even closer, and he burrowed her ripe curves to the angular saddle of his hips. When Burke let himself fall backward, Dale instinctively clutched his right shoulder as they went down. With her right hand she cushioned her descent so as not to crush Burke's back to the hard deck.

His hands slid upward to curve themselves about her small waist; then he lifted her body to guide it carefully so that she was kneeling astride him. Dale's breath was shocked out of her body at the feelings whirling in heady turbulence through her. When she spoke, her voice was hoarse with longing.

"The deck is cold. Let me get a blanket."

She started to rise, but his hands pulled her back down and his voice was threaded with husky amusement as he said, "You'll keep me warm. The contrast between your delicious heat and the cold deck is quite erotic."

Dale was grateful that her face was in shadows and that Burke couldn't see the flush on her cheeks that extended rapidly downward at his seductive words. But as his hands moved lower to her thighs and caressed with deliberate, circular motions, all coherent thought fled.

She leaned forward, sliding her knees toward his

shoulders so that her derriere was supported by his legs, bent at the knees, and her own, hugging his taut flanks. She let her flowing hair caress and surround his head and neck in a silky midnight veil, and Burke took his hand off one of her thighs to grip a handful of the fragrant tresses, then buried his face in them, inhaling the clean scent with obvious enjoyment.

Bending closer to him, Dale supported her weight on her elbows, which she placed on his tensing biceps, and let her breasts brush against his chest, her body absorbing tiny shocks as her nipples tingled at the slight grazing of the crinkly golden hair on his chest. She rubbed her breasts lightly against the male nipples, emboldened by the groan that erupted from deep within Burke's chest and vibrated against her own.

His hands slid along the outer curves of her body, mapping the arcs and indentations as they slid upward in lazy quest of her breasts. As his fingers stroked her velvety midriff in the small space between their bodies, then ascended to cup the fullness of the creamy globes, kneading them gently, Dale's breath came in jagged spurts.

She arched her body over Burke's to allow him easy access to her upper body, and lowered her head to drop kisses along his jawline, delighting in the rough, bristly feel against her parted lips. She teased him as she moved fleetingly over his face, placing butterfly kisses on his forehead, eyes, and nose until an impatient hand came up and anchored her head to allow him full possession of her mouth. His tongue separated her lips with savage need and plundered the sweet honey inside while his other hand continued its lazy massage of her breast, then switched to the other voluptuous globe. As he began to narrow the circumference of his caresses, restricting them now to the taut areola around her nipple, Dale felt the blood coursing scaldingly to every nerve center in her body.

His fingers closed about the tip of one breast, rolling it smoothly with lazy deliberation and then pinching it gently before moving to its tumescent twin. His mouth covered hers, swallowing her helpless moan. Dale moved restlessly, instinctively seeking release from the pleasure-pain, and Burke again closed his hands about her waist, placing her gently above his rising manhood.

As their bodies met in the most intimate way, Dale felt the muscles in Burke's body go rigid. His hands slid to her buttocks, cupping them firmly, guiding her tentative movements until she set her own rhythm and opened herself to receive him deeper.

She moved slightly forward, and Burke's mouth fastened on her breasts, sucking on their fullness until Dale thought she would go wild with the aching throbbing he elicited in her innermost recesses. His lips closed on the crimson crests, and his teeth nibbled sharply.

"You taste so good," he told her thickly against a pulsating peak, making the flame of need burn ever brighter into a conflagration of yearning passion.

Their rhythm accelerated by silent, natural consent, hot flesh moving against hot flesh until Dale could stand the added torment of his mouth and teeth no longer and rested her heaving breasts against the broad musculature of his torso, resting her head on his shoulder. As his hands continued their kneading and massaging of her buttocks, pressing her even closer to himself, Dale moved her tongue lightly over the corded intersection where his neck and shoulders joined. Then she drew the moist, salty flesh into her mouth, nipping sharply, and felt him shudder underneath her and within her.

His body arched upward into hers until Dale felt as if they had been molded into one searing entity. His fingers dug into her skin, locking her to him, increasing the tempo of their thrusting so that Dale lost all sense of time and place. She felt as though she were in the center of a whirlpool, her body thrumming and thrashing in his grip, responding to his guidance, bending to his will.

His exquisite, deep stroking created sensual shivers in the very core of her, and the shivers turned into spasms that rippled through her body, cascading in her loins, propelling her into a liquid spiral of emotion in which the two of them were the only reality. Dale clung to Burke as the only stable, solid anchor in her shimmering world of desire.

Abruptly, she felt him go rigid beneath her. His arms circled her body like iron manacles, his teeth gently biting into the marble slope of her shoulder, as he, too, was carried to the pinnacle of sensation. At the peak of fulfillment, Burke groaned her name, and the deep sound merged with her cry of joy. He held her tightly to him as they battled the crest of the mountainous wave that tossed them and pounded them in a storm of pleasure. Their ragged breathing filled the summer night, their bodies' own fragrance mingling with those of the river, and their hearts beat rapidly in unison as they lay entangled for a long time, riding out the storm of their passion.

When Burke moved, Dale moaned her protest, wanting to remain joined to him forever. He caressed her back and flanks with smoothing strokes, soothing her with indecipherable murmurings as his hands gently quieted her.

Dale sighed her pleasure and shifted her body slightly to be able to nibble on his neck and throat, savoring the smell and texture of his skin. Burke responded with quick love bites that chased chills up and down her spine. Then he whispered softly to her, his warm breath an erotic tingle against the pink shell of her ear.

"It's getting cold. Let's go inside."

"Not yet," she protested, not wanting to disrupt the beauty of the moment. The lovemaking had been intense for both of them, Burke deliberately slowing the tempo so that when their fulfillment came, the force was devastating.

But for her their union had been more than physical. Never had she felt such complete communion before, and her total giving of herself had been far more than sexual.

His hands stroked her back, from her thighs to her neck, and this time his touch was one of passionate possession. "I don't want you getting ill on me. Your back's turning to ice."

"So let's reverse our positions," she tempted him throatily.

She could feel him harden within her, but his iron self-control came into play again.

"We'll do that, lady. But not up here. Below, I'll let you pick any position you want."

A cool breeze played on her moist, exposed skin, but the shudder that gripped her body was induced by more than the cold. She'd been careful not to confess her love to Burke during their lovemaking. But she'd hoped for a more tender endearment than *lady*. Somehow she hated it when he called her that, as if negating her individuality and importance to him.

Burke felt her shudder and gently but swiftly pushed her away from him, severing their union and rising. He bent to pick her up, and Dale curled her body into his, burrowing against him for more than warmth. For just an instant she'd been terrified. The ruthless way he'd separated their joining had shown her that Burke had not changed. . . . Perhaps she'd just romanticized her view of him to justify her decision to give herself to him.

Burke mistook her clinging for a search for body warmth, and he pressed her harder against him, quickening his pace to the ladder.

He took her to his own bedroom but Dale couldn't see much in the darkness, where a rectangle of moonlight was the only illumination. Softly depositing her on the bed by the window, Burke joined her, carefully lowering his body onto hers. His eyes gleamed opalescent for a second in the moonlight before he dipped his head, saying against her passion-swollen lips, "I'm open to any suggestions. You tell me what position you prefer and we'll try it."

But his mouth closed over hers to drive all lucid thought from her head, and she followed his lead with the malleability of love.

She whispered her love for him silently as his fingers whispered over her skin, and the cool breeze from the open window enveloped their straining bodies with its fragrant embrace . . .

- 8 -

DALE STRETCHED, FEELING the sun's warmth on her eyelids but reluctant to fully wake up. She felt too languorous and fulfilled to move. The night of inventive lovemaking flashed through her mind, and she smiled with feline pleasure. Burke had not been wrong when he'd said he made as good a student as teacher.

Hunger for his touch and his voice made her open her eyes, and she reached for him as she turned her head.

He wasn't there.

She trained her nostrils to detect breakfast. Since they'd skipped dinner altogether and Burke had the biggest appetite she'd ever witnessed, it stood to reason that he'd be cooking breakfast. But no appetizing aromas drifted to her from the kitchen.

As she reluctantly got up from the bed, which still smelled of Burke and their combined essence, Dale began to feel uneasy. When Burke had carried her over the threshold of his room last night, her thoughts had been on him, not the room; and besides, it had been too dark to see much anyway. Yet, she'd had some vague sense of clutter, of his belongings strewn about. And now the room was bare.

She walked over to the dresser and found it empty. No suitcase was visible, nor any other article of clothing or anything that could have belonged to him, including his fishing equipment.

She ran to her bedroom to get a robe, then raced to the kitchen. She called his name, trying to fight the panic that was threatening to overwhelm her. Nothing could have happened to Burke.

Nothing had.

A note was propped against a vase in which wild flowers flaunted their dramatic beauty, permeating the room with their strong scent. She read it aloud, as if the sound of her voice would drive away the ensuing nightmare.

Dale:

I'm sorry to leave like this, but I think it's best I do so. I guess you were right when you resisted our chemistry. One night with you made it damn hard to contemplate returning to Saudi Arabia. If I'd stayed longer, something stronger might have developed, and the sites I work in are no fit place for a woman, especially one with a promising career of her own. Forgive me—I feel like a heel, but a clean break is best. You know how to handle the *Seaprincess* now, so I don't have to worry about your getting hurt.

I'm leaving a map on which I've circled places that may be of interest to you as you finish your vacation.

Good-bye, sweet lady.

Burke

The slight swaying of the boat under her feet proved too much for Dale. While it had added to the excitement of their lovemaking the night before, now it only signified the instability of her world. A world that had begun spinning away from her. A world that had no borders and that threatened to suck her into its cruel void.

She sank down onto a kitchen chair, recalling the first time she'd sat in this same chair when she'd tried to persuade Burke to leave. Her mind played back snatches of memory, particles of her experiences with Burke that evolved into a broken, painful kaleidoscope of remembrances.

Trying to fight the pain that wrenched at her heart and was impeding her breathing, Dale forced herself to read the note again. Hysterical laughter bubbled in her throat as she came to his statement that he didn't have to worry about her getting hurt. Was that a rationalization to ease his own conscience? Did he really think his abrupt leaving would not affect her? Did he really have so little sensitivity that he hadn't known his departure would shatter her heart?

Tears began to blur her vision, but Dale refused to shed them. She had no one to blame but herself. She could have been less stubborn. She could have agreed to leave the *Seaprincess*.

She sighed as she let the note float to the table.

Burke had not pointed a gun at her and forced her into his bed. She'd invited him to make love to her. She'd decided to take the chance.

And look where it had gotten her.

With the refined fury that only raw, unendurable hurt can induce, Dale took the flowers from the vase and crushed them. A momentary twinge of guilt assailed her at the destruction of such beauty, but the small gesture helped to discharge some of her hurt.

Her hatred was only beginning.

Determined not to let Burke drive her away from the last few days of her vacation, Dale stuffed the flowers in the garbage and quickly made for her bedroom. There she found a pair of slacks and a long-sleeved blouse, and after torturing her hair into a top-knot, she took some books and a bathing suit and left the bedroom again.

She intended to finish this vacation on her own if it killed her. She didn't know much about cleaning fish, but as she opened the refrigerator to get some juice and saw the fresh catch from yesterday, she determined that she would learn before the day was over.

Damn Burke and his insidious charm! His looks alone she'd have been able to resist, albeit with some difficulty. But she had foolishly allowed herself to believe that Burke had more depth than Joel.

He didn't. He was just as shallow. Only more cunning. And calculating. He'd gotten what he wanted from her, and had left her to return to his precious job.

She'd been wrong in her assessment. And how easy she'd made it for him.

But although her pride smarted, it was nothing

compared to the anguish that clawed at her insides over his smooth deception. There hadn't been this bleak, abrading sense of loss over her breakup with Joel.

Burke had not, of course, known of her love. But his callous, cruel departure had turned her surrender into something stained, ugly. She felt used. The beauty of their union was marred.

A violent sob twisted its way to her throat, burning it. She pushed down the bile, refusing to break down.

She wouldn't cry. Burke was not worth it. He'd taken something beautiful and killed it before it had a chance at fruition.

No, she would not cry. She would survive.

"I really am sorry about the mix-up," Wyatt Martin told her three days later. "When Burke stopped by to pay his bill, he told me he had to go back to work sooner than he'd anticipated and that he got off at one of the Missouri ports."

"He did," Dale said, plastering a smile on her pale face through sheer effort. Even hearing Burke's name caused gut-wrenching pain. Over the last few days, she had given herself several pep talks, but the hurt ran deep. She opened her purse to pay the remaining half of her bill, but Wyatt shrugged her money aside.

"Put that away. After the inconvenience we unwittingly caused you, you've got a refund coming."

He began writing out a check, but Dale stopped him. His office had caused more than inconvenience. But Wyatt could not have known how stupid she'd be.

"Don't, please. At least let me pay half the bill. I did get to have the *Seaprincess* to myself for a while."

Her right hand, which had shot out in an instinctive gesture to stop him from writing the check, was shaking. Dale hid it in her lap, lacing her fingers to stop their trembling.

Wyatt's shrewd hazel eyes rested on her face, taking in the pallor of her skin, which not even a heavy application of makeup could hide. She usually wore little makeup, but after three nights of almost no sleep and days of frenetic exploring and swimming, mauve shadows ringed her eyes, and her mint-green irises lacked their usual luster.

"Are you all right?" Wyatt asked gently.

"Fine," Dale insisted. "I just got carried away, being skipper of the *Seaprincess*. Old Man River is very seductive, and I found myself trying to do too much and eating too little."

"Is that all there was?"

Dale's eyes began to flash with ire. She was not too pleased with the male sex at the moment, and she never liked anyone interfering in her private business. Wyatt Martin might have rented her the houseboat, but his role in her life ended here and now.

"I appreciate your renting the *Seaprincess* to me on such short notice, and I'm sorry if you had cause to worry when I wasn't here for the orientation," she said briskly.

Following her lead, he got up and came around his desk to stand in front of her. The sun imbued everything with hurtful brightness, and Wyatt's hair gleamed a rich chestnut.

"I think I may have more cause to worry now. Did Burke make a pass at you?"

Dale was tempted to turn on her heel and leave,

but she recognized the genuine concern in Wyatt's deep voice.

"Several, I'd say. But I didn't take them seriously. I suppose making passes is as natural to him as breathing."

Wyatt didn't contradict her statement. He leaned against the edge of his mahogany desk and told her softly, "I've never known Burke to run before."

Her gaze flew to his; then, disconcerted at the compassion she read there, she quickly looked away, concentrating instead on the Mississippi, visible from the window that made up one whole wall.

"I—I don't know what you mean," she mumbled.

"Burke has always taken his full vacation, come hell or high water. Although he likes women, he made it clear that he preferred to houseboat alone this time, so the fact that he took such pains to convince you to share the *Seaprincess* with him means that his feelings were more involved than they usually are."

"Burke doesn't have any feelings," Dale said bitterly. Then, realizing what she'd let escape, she tried to backtrack. "Listen, I appreciate your concern, but I'm a grown woman. I can take care of myself."

"It's precisely because you *are* a grown woman— a striking, desirable woman—that I'm concerned. I'm just sorry he got to you first. There wouldn't be that pain in those beautiful green eyes if *I* had accompanied you."

"Such confidence. You men are all alike. You think the sun rises and sets on you."

He straightened and took her hand in his.

"That's not true. Don't paint us all with the same brush. I *do* mean it. I wish Burke hadn't gotten there first. Because I know that now I don't stand a chance with you. And I wish it weren't too late for me."

She heard the deep conviction in his voice and tried to smile. "You're right. I'm sorry. I shouldn't generalize. But I've acted very unwisely, and it feels so much better to direct all the bitterness, and even part of the blame, onto someone else."

"My shoulders are big. How about letting fly some of that hurt at me. Who knows? You might find I'm a very likable fellow."

She laughed, a weak, uncertain sound. But it lifted her spirits, because it showed that she was coping. Or, at least, beginning to cope.

"I'm grateful for the offer, but I wouldn't be good company right now."

"You're allowed to take a raincheck," he suggested, grinning, as he accompanied her to the door.

Dale smiled at him, finding that this time the smile was not so hard to produce. Wyatt looked so handsome in his dark slacks and light-green shirt, his eyes interested, his expression open. But she'd been deceived before and she was not anxious for anyone's company but her own for a while.

"I don't think so," she said, smiling to take the sting out of her rejection. "I'll be leaving the state, so I think it's better if we say good-bye now."

"You're running away, too?"

She looked at him sharply, not liking the implication.

"Burke wouldn't have left the houseboat so soon if he hadn't been afraid of something," Wyatt elaborated. "And your leaving the state smacks of the same thing."

Some of her anger returned. "I don't think that's

for you to say. You really don't have the right to meddle in my affairs, but I'll tell you this much: I had a job offer in another state even before boarding the *Seaprincess*. As a matter of fact, that was one of the reasons I wanted to take this vacation—to think over the offer."

As she opened the door and stepped outside, his quiet words followed her.

"But I bet the new job didn't take on such desirable qualities until Burke beat a hasty retreat."

Dale opened her mouth to deny his charge, but found she couldn't in all honesty do so. She hadn't been sure if she'd take the new job, but all of a sudden it seemed imperative to accept it.

With a curt good-bye, she left Wyatt and his knowing, sympathetic eyes. She didn't need any men at this point in her life—particularly men who asked probing, uncomfortable questions.

As it turned out, Dale did see Wyatt Martin again. They went out to dinner several times before her move to St. Louis. Despite the fact that he was deeply attracted to her, he'd pleaded the case of his friend, telling her that this was probably one time when Burke had been faced with too much emotion, too much involvement. And Burke hadn't known how to deal with it, except to retreat.

But Dale was neither satisfied with Wyatt's theory nor inclined to believe it. She knew Burke's passion for his work. And he was too self-sufficient to let anyone come to mean very much to him. He'd guarded his heart carefully for too long to let any woman inside it. Dale might have bridged some of his defenses, but if he'd really loved her, or felt anything deep and lasting for her at all, he'd have returned. Or at least would have tried to contact her, called her, written to her. Anything.

There had been no word from him in two months.

Now, settled in her new job and about ready to move into a bigger apartment than the studio the company had secured for her until she found permanent quarters, Dale was continuing in her battle to forget Burke Sheridan.

He was never far from her thoughts, especially in the quiet, long hours of the night. But she'd learned to push him away from her mind, treating his memory like a bad habit she had to get rid of.

Determined to keep busy beyond the hectic hours she put in on her new job, Dale decided to explore her new home. She felt homesickness for Iowa, and for her parents and friends. Despite her protests, her parents had come along to help her move. Her father, a retired college professor not used to inactivity, made life quite hard for her mother. But Laurel Hayward was already plotting to find activities to keep Rodney occupied while she was at her job, conducting management seminars. Laurel had welcomed the opportunity to help her daughter settle in her studio apartment, as well as to give Rodney something to do.

But Dale's parents had only stayed a few days and had been gone for weeks. And although Laurel had sensed there was something wrong, she hadn't pressed Dale for an explanation.

So Dale had taken advantage of the last days of summer to travel along the Great River Road system, which took her either north or south along the Missouri or Illinois shores of the Big Muddy. She visited Mark

Twain's boyhood home in Hannibal, experiencing a moment of joy at seeing that the white picket fence was still there.

She also explored Elsah, a tiny village with fairy-tale qualities, and Grafton, where many of the residents constructed their homes on stilts to escape the flooding river.

When summer began to give way to autumn, Dale confined her travels to the area near Jefferson National Expansion Memorial, where the glittering Gateway Arch dominated the skyscape.

She learned that St. Louis had been founded in 1764 as a trading post by Pierre Laclède, and had earned the nickname the "Paris of the West." Laclède's Landing, a nine-block area squeezed between Eads Bridge and the Martin Luther King, Jr., Bridge, had been recently revamped, its rundown warehouses converted to a commercial and entertainment spot. As she walked about one Sunday, admiring the cast-iron columns and facades—remnants of a time when St. Louis led in the manufacture of structural cast iron—red brick buildings with limestone moldings and intricately arched windows, Dale couldn't help wishing Burke were here with her.

She fought off the feeling, realizing that his memory was never far from the surface of her consciousness, and decided to keep her mind even more actively occupied. Her visits to the St. Louis Art Museum, with its collection of ancient, Oriental, Near Eastern, Oceanic, pre-Columbian, and Impressionist art, helped. So did her fascinating excursion into history at the Museum of Westward Expansion, featuring a progression through the nineteenth century peopled by Indians, explorers, trappers, traders, and settlers.

Her anger and hurt still remained, but she felt better about taking a positive approach to life. Burke had left her, and she'd had no say in that. But she did have a choice in how she conducted her life, now that he was no longer a part of it, and she chose to fill it with knowledge and beauty, rather than spend it languishing at home for someone who'd probably forgotten all about her.

The following Saturday was the big day. Dale hired some movers to make the switch from her studio apartment to the larger one she'd rented with a purchase option. The day was a blustery one, the sky a peculiar taupe tone with only a hint of rose in it.

Dale got up early and dressed warmly in the woolen slacks and the flame-red cashmere sweater she'd laid out the night before. After supervising the loading of her furniture onto the truck, she went back to the apartment for one last look.

Checking the bathroom cabinet one last time, she was ready to return the key to the landlord. As she was leaving the tiny room, she heard masculine steps outside the front door and dug into the side pockets of her slacks for the key, thinking it was her landlord anticipating her.

But as she stepped into the bedroom-living room and saw who was dwarfing the small area with his large, imposing presence, she froze.

Burke.

They stared at each other silently for long, hungry minutes. Dale felt his visual exploration with palpable intensity.

She tore her gaze away from his and paled as she noticed what he was holding in his hands: an exact small-scale replica of the *Seaprincess*. Just the sight of the exquisitely executed houseboat, its every detail and shade of color captured, brought a huge lump to her throat and unaccustomed moistness to her eyes.

But then the painful memories of ten weeks ago resurfaced, drowning out the incipient pleasure of seeing Burke again, of being transported for just an instant to the boat that had brought them together and had seen the blossoming and then withering of her love.

Welcome, bracing anger replaced her shock and swept away her momentary weakness.

"I don't know how you found out where I live, Burke, but as you can see, I am just leaving."

He took a step forward, but she sidestepped him neatly and headed for the door. He extended a hand, but she steered clear of it as if it were a deadly menace. Which, in a very real way, Burke *was*. A menace to her well-being, to her sanity. She was taking charge of her life and was fighting for every vestige of control. She would not let him get her down again.

"Good-bye, Burke."

"Dale, I need to talk to you."

His urgent, deep tone would have had her melting two months ago. Now it only raised the level of her rage.

"This *lady*"—she had the pleasure of seeing him wince as she emphasized the word—"has nothing to say to you. You had me at your disposal for an extra three days this past summer, but you chose not to exercise that option. Whatever you may have to say to me now holds no interest for me."

She walked out the door, heading for the landlord's apartment. Burke followed, his long legs permitting him to keep up with her easily.

"I realize you have reason to be upset at me, Dale, but I'm asking you to give me a chance to explain." Holding out the beautiful model of the *Seaprincess*, he added, "And to take this peace offering."

"Should I give you the chance you gave me when you stole away from my side like a thief in the night, leaving only a note?" she said, turning on him with a fury that was fairly spilling over. She took a deep breath to maintain control. She would *not* fall apart in front of him. "Oh, yes, you left a bouquet of flowers as well. I guess I ought to be thankful you didn't leave me any money. But the point is," she went on, gesturing at the model of the houseboat, "I don't want any more mementos from you."

"This is not a souvenir, Dale," Burke said quietly. "I had it made because I realized what an idiot I'd been—"

"And since you're back in town, you figured your offering would sweeten me up and we'd be back to square one? Forget it, Burke. I may be trusting, and I take full responsibility for my actions, including instigating our lovemaking"—she paused and knocked on the landlord's door—"but I didn't deserve the kind of cowardly treatment I received from you."

"I plead guilty to emotional cowardice, but—" He stopped as the landlord opened the door and Dale returned the key. After receiving the security deposit from the man, Dale told him good-bye and headed for the front door.

Burke tried to stop her, grabbing her arm.

She snatched it back. "I'm very busy today, Burke. I don't have time for you."

His eyes glittered with annoyance. "Then you'll just have to *make* time."

She threw the long braid that was resting on her left side back over her shoulder in a nervous, angry gesture.

"Leave me alone, Burke. I have a very hectic day ahead of me. And I don't appreciate your being troublesome."

A muscle twitched in his jaw, but he was once more in control.

"I'll help you."

His calm assurance stung. "No, thanks! I can manage quite well without you."

Before he could answer, she flung the outside door open and stepped through. Ignoring his urgent repetition of her name, she got into her car and drove away with an unaccustomed squeal of tires.

- 9 -

DALE DROVE ALONG at breakneck speed, and by the time she reached her new apartment, she felt cooled down and able to cope once more. She didn't even want to speculate on the reason for Burke's being in St. Louis. She had too much to do today, and thoughts of Burke were not conducive to organized, constructive labor.

She looked at the apartment house with pleasure. Its uncluttered lines and Spanish flavor gave it an airiness that was very welcome after the cramped quarters she'd just vacated. And her oversize furniture—she needed large furniture for her long frame—would certainly fare better in the new place.

The movers, who had left her old apartment before she did, were now arriving. She smiled grimly, thinking that she'd certainly given them a run for their money.

But her smile disappeared as she saw who was

approaching from across the street.

Burke. With the miniature *Seaprincess* tucked under his arm.

She wished she could get into her car again and lead Burke on a wild-goose chase. Hopefully lose him along the River Road.

But Burke was too tenacious to get left behind. And too smart to get lost. And then there were the movers, who had apparently said something and were now impatiently repeating it while she stared like a hopeless idiot at the muscular form in brown slacks and honey-gold sweater crossing the street.

"Yes, I'll go ahead and open the door," she told them absently as she tried to gather her wits together. Bulldog or not, Burke was going to find out he could not corner her.

Burke followed her silently into the new apartment, not saying anything, generally staying out of the way after putting the houseboat model in the kitchen. Dale supposed she could have asked the burly men to remove him, but that smacked too much of insecurity. She'd get rid of him on her own.

Bringing in her gigantic couch, a nine-foot monstrosity with upholstery showing wild maroon leaves on a gold background, did necessitate Burke's help. The movers had a problem getting the couch through the tall but thin door—she'd had to leave her couch in her boss's garage until now—and Burke stepped in, adding his brawn and brains to the project.

Although Dale asked him with a patently false smile to leave, Burke ignored her and suggested they try the back door. Without replying, Dale went to unpack some boxes in her kitchen, where she resolutely kept her eyes from the lovely replica of the *Seaprincess*.

A few struggling, cursing minutes later, three disheveled men appeared at her front door again.

Dale went to greet them and grinned maliciously at Burke.

"Having trouble?"

One of the movers scowled at her and told her, "Lady, you're paying us by the hour, and the way it's going, this will be the only place we move today. You better prepare to empty your savings account."

Dale overlooked his bad manners, having had experience with movers before and sympathizing with their efforts to solve this space puzzle.

"How about if we chop the sofa up into small pieces and paste it up later?" Burke said mildly as they all recovered their breaths.

The other mover's eyes sparkled. "Now, there's an idea."

"Hold it, fellows," Dale said before the idea snowballed.

"What about giving this to a truly needy organization and I buy you a brand-new sofa?" Burke asked her, moving away from the couch and slowly straightening his back. His sweater was smudged in several places, and his blond hair covered his broad forehead and one quizzical eyebrow.

"That suggestion is typical of your throwaway philosophy of life," Dale said sharply. "Frankly, *I*'d rather throw *you* away. The couch, at least, has staying power."

His eyes glittered angrily, and a muscle moved spasmodically in his jaw. But before he could reply, one of the movers wearily said, "If you two lovebirds can put off your quarreling until after we're done, do you think we can get on with this?"

Burke turned back to the couch again, squaring his shoulders as if going into battle. Dale watched as all three men resumed their waltz, shifting the couch first one way, then the other, always coming up short. Finally, they hit on a certain angle, rotating the couch ninety degrees and practically standing it on one end, which seemed to work. Unfortunately, one of the men got his hand caught between couch and door, and he let go of the couch with a loud yelp.

Burke bore the brunt of the burden, and Dale instinctively rushed up to help. As the other mover pushed forward, unable to stop the momentum and catching Burke off guard, the couch did finally scrape and stumble its way in.

But not before Burke lost his footing and fell flat on his back, with Dale on top of him and part of the endless couch on top of her.

"Are you all right?" Burke wheezed out, his tone and eyes anxious.

Dale nodded weakly. At least her spine wasn't broken.

Burke began barking out orders, and the two other men were able to lift the couch sufficiently so he could slide out from underneath the monolith and bring Dale out with him.

Despite her hoarse protests, Burke quickly picked her up and carried her out of harm's way into the kitchen, where he proceeded to run his hands over her limbs and body, feeling for broken bones and ribs. The dull red that suffused his cheekbones at this intimate contact told her Burke was excited; obviously his libido was never out of commission, no matter what the circumstances. The same could not be said for her: Even if she had not been so gloriously angry at him, the numbness in her whole body would have kept her from experiencing any arousal.

"You'll live," he told her finally, but despite his dry tone and impassive face, she could tell he was very relieved. Probably didn't want to be hit with a lawsuit, she thought cynically. At least her thought processes were unimpeded—she was experiencing too much pleasure being angry at Burke to be deprived of *that* emotion.

"Stay there," he ordered on the heels of his terse pronouncement. "I'll take care of the rest of the moving."

He left the kitchen, ostensibly to go supervise the rest of the operation—child's play, now that the couch was inside the apartment. Ignoring his command, Dale immediately got off the marble counter and followed in his wake.

The movers were bringing in the last piece of furniture, Dale saw as she paused at the end of the hallway, feeling suddenly weak and queasy. But watching Burke pay and tip the movers galvanized her into action.

"What do you think you're doing?" she asked in a low, furious voice. To her dismay, the movers beat a hasty retreat.

"Paying the movers," he told her laconically. "And I added a generous tip. You must admit that their job today was above and beyond the call of duty."

She looked around angrily, pivoting several times as she missed seeing her purse in the red haze of fury. She finally located it by the door and rummaged violently for her wallet, eventually locating it and jerking out a wad of bills.

She handed the bills to him. "Now, get out of here.

I told you I don't need you, and I just want—"

"At this moment I don't give a da—a darn what you want." The sound that came out of his lips was certainly not the beginning for *darn,* but evidently Burke could still exert some control over himself. "I want to make sure you're all right."

"Aren't you a little late with this exalted concern?" she told him coldly. "Don't worry, I'll be fine. Women have to have excellent survival skills with men like you and—" She broke off, not willing to regale Burke with her previous experience with Joel. Joel was part of her past. Just as Burke was.

"Now, will you please leave?" she added, turning to leave him.

"Don't you turn your back on me," he growled, grabbing her arm and spinning her around.

She was shocked. That was the closest thing to a raised voice she'd ever heard from Burke.

"Why not?" she said, taunting him. "You turned your back on me. Do you want me to write you a dismissal note? Will that make it clearer to you that I want you out of my life?"

His other hand came up to close about her arm. "You'd test the patience of a saint," he snapped, the pitch of his voice deepening until it seemed to vibrate through her.

"And you're no saint, are you, Burke?" she flung at him, giving free rein to her hurt and hatred. She'd been half living the previous months. Now she felt vibrantly, painfully, alive. "You're an opportunist and—"

But she was not allowed to finish her sentence as Burke hauled her against him. He let go of her arms to imprison her head in his hands, and the initial force of his action made her lose her balance and fall against him. His mouth crushed hers, grinding her lips against her teeth, but even as she began registering some pain, the bruising pressure eased, becoming gentler, more seductive in nature.

The touch of his fingers on her face lightened, too, turning into soft caresses that two months ago would have had her dissolving against him. But the unexpected violence of his kiss had made her wary. She stood leaning against him, without offering any resistance but without softening, either. Her cold withdrawal had a quicker effect than a struggle would have and he lifted his head, looking into her eyes with frustrated passion and puzzlement.

"You can't have gone cold on me in only two months," he said flatly, challenging her lack of response.

"No?" she said, angered anew by his conceit. "What was there to fan the flames? After leaving me that heartless note suggesting a complete break between us, you made no effort to get in touch with me for two months."

A flash of triumph lit his eyes briefly. "I realize you're furious at me and have every right to be so. But I know you haven't forgotten me—"

"Think again. I began forgetting you as soon as I read that note. I even went out with your charming, *decent* friend, Wyatt Martin."

"If you were totally over me, you wouldn't keep harping on my note," he said complacently. Her eyes filled with fury, and he added, "And I know you're not serious about Wyatt. I talked to him and Wyatt said he couldn't get to first base with you. I also talked to your parents—"

Her eyes widened with indignation. "You talked to my parents? And you discussed me with Wyatt? How could you ... you—you—" Words failed her.

"Wyatt was concerned about you," Burke said, raking a hand through his hair. "He drove home a few unpleasant truths before he'd divulge your address ..."

"I'm sure the distinction makes all the difference," she said sarcastically. Suddenly weary from the shock of seeing him, of having a couch fall on her, and of his brutal kiss, she said, "Burke, please leave. I may have thought ill of you before, but after what you just did and said, you've hit rock bottom in my esteem and I never want to see you again."

He took her hand in his and caressed it, retaining his hold despite her violent pulling. "I'll change your opinion of me. I'll make you forgive my temporary insanity."

She succeeded in tearing her hand away and told him, "For the last time, Burke, get out of my life."

"I want you to come with me to Saudi Arabia."

"You're crazy," she accused after the first stunned moment.

"You're right. I'm crazy about you and want you with me."

"And I'm supposed to leave all this"—she waved her hand wildly at her new place—"and my job, and just traipse after you?"

"For a short while. Then I intend to—"

"I could care less what you intend," she told him, stalking to the door. "Out!"

He stiffened but began walking to the door. "I know you've had a great shock today, so I'll leave for now. But I'll be back."

"Not here, you won't," she said, gritting her teeth.

"I'll see you tomorrow. I have to return to Saudi Arabia shortly, so I don't have much time." With that he dropped a kiss on her nose and left.

Dale stared at his retreating back, shaking her head at his audacity. Then, as she slowly turned to tackle the unpleasant chore of unpacking myriad boxes and crates, she saw the miniature *Seaprincess,* looking impossibly fragile as it sat on one of the cushions of the gargantuan couch.

Burke had not only left behind very vivid vestiges of his presence: his masculine scent and lemony cologne on her clothes, the imprint of his kiss on her still-tender lips, the imprint of his body's insistent pressure against hers. He'd also left a physical reminder of himself and of everything she'd tried to forget over the past several weeks.

Pain and memory rushed back with equal force, a heavy chain around her chest. She picked up the exquisite reproduction from the couch and heaved it high in the air, unaware of its weight. He had known instinctively what this memento would mean to her, and she intended to crush it, to destroy it, as she herself had felt destroyed only a few short months ago.

But as she brought her arm down, her fingers would not release their death hold on the *Seaprincess.* Instead, her other arm came up slowly to cradle the houseboat against her chest and neck while burning tears gathered in her eyes, then overflowed.

Fighting her tears and memories with gritty determination, Dale swathed the *Seaprincess* in crinkly paper, then put it in a large bag and set it inside a closet. She could not bring herself to destroy such a beautiful work of art, she told herself.

But neither would she torture herself with a constant reminder of Burke or their brief, doomed shipboard romance.

- *10* -

KNOWING BURKE WOULD make good his promise to return, Dale quickly dealt with her unpacking. She put the most urgent things away—clothes, books— while leaving many utensils for later. She would finish unpacking once Burke was safely out of town.

Quickly packing a suitcase, Dale paused to make a phone call before taking a shower. She called her boss and told him that she'd be doing the legwork on the new resort this weekend instead of the next week-end. Harvey Nesmond seemed a bit surprised at her schedule change, since he'd given her Monday off to get settled. But Dale was able to convince him that it would be advisable for her to work on the project sooner rather than later. Harvey generally allowed her the freedom and autonomy to conduct her job as she saw fit, with the understanding that he expected results and satisfied clients. Beyond that, he did not keep a close eye on his executives.

So Dale left for the new resort near Hannibal, Mark Twain's boyhood home, and took her briefcase along to get caught up on some paperwork. She didn't return until four days later.

Expecting to find some note or irate communication from Burke, she was thrown off balance when she opened her door and saw nothing. She began getting angry again, thinking that perhaps he hadn't even meant what he'd said. He might not have shown up after all.

But despite Burke's wild, evasive nature, she didn't think he'd lied. She still credited him with *some* integrity. Burke might be an adventurer, but having said he would come the following day, he undoubtedly had. Perhaps he'd been so angry at finding her gone that he'd just stormed away. Perhaps he'd taken her at her word and left for good this time.

Somehow, this line of thought gave Dale none of the satisfaction she'd anticipated.

During the next four weeks, Dale ran herself into the ground. She worked late hours at the office, then came home and threw all her energies into decorating her new residence. By November, she had lost some weight. Not only was she burning up more calories with her frenzied schedule, but she found herself eating less. Unfortunately, now that she could afford to eat all she wanted, her appetite seemed to have deserted her. Nor did she take any pleasure in buying new clothes to fit her now-streamlined figure—shopping was just one more activity to fill the time and the emptiness she felt inside.

Her washing machine had perished on her, and she'd had to purchase a new one. But since they didn't have a chocolate-brown one to match her brand-new dryer, a house-warming present from her parents, she put in an order for one, and in the meantime had to endure the inconvenience of going to a Laundromat for a while.

This particular Saturday morning as she headed out to her car with the week's laundry, she began to wish she had bought one of the available washing machines instead of holding out for the color she wanted. The temperature was in the twenties, colder than usual for mid-November, and the strong wind had the velocity of a hurricane.

This weather certainly wasn't helping her morale, Dale reflected as she slammed the trunk door on her laundry basket and got into the driver's seat of her car. To cheer herself up, she put on an ABBA tape. They could raise the spirit of the living dead, she thought. This morbid comparison brought to mind the one magical evening she had spent with Burke, when she'd begun getting glimpses into his complex personality.

Forcefully driving all thought of Burke away, Dale made herself concentrate on the words of the upbeat songs... *"Take a chance...one man, one woman..."*

The sentiments brought tears to her eyes, and she quickly turned off the tape. The words seemed like musical mockery, and apparently, on this gray, gloomy morning her defenses were especially low. Skipping breakfast, a meal she didn't ordinarily enjoy, had not been a good idea, either. She was asking a lot of her body lately, and she needed to refuel it if she expected it to function adequately.

Coming to a sudden decision, Dale stopped at a

pancake house. The cheerful, noisy atmosphere created by families laughing and enjoying themselves was double-edged. While it made her smile in unconscious response, it also drove home the reminder that she would not share another breakfast with Burke.

A young waitress approached her, the inevitable coffeepot in her hand, as soon as she sat down. "Want some coffee?"

Dale smiled at the bubbly young woman, envying her vitality and good humor. "Yes, please. And I'd like to order right away, too, if you don't mind."

After giving her order, Dale cupped her cold hands around the hot porcelain coffee cup, too lost in her thoughts to feel self-conscious about being the only unaccompanied person in the room. When a shadow dropped across her table, she paid it no attention, thinking the waitress had come to bring her some fresh water.

But a body followed the shadow, and as she heard the scrape of a chair being dragged across the floor and creaking under someone's weight, she absently raised her gaze. If some man thought she was an easy pickup, she would tell him plainly that she wasn't interested.

But the words never left her mouth. Her gaze widened as she met Burke's mocking glance.

"What—what are you doing here?" Dale wondered if she could possibly be hallucinating. After all, hadn't she been fighting Burke's persistent, bittersweet memory only minutes ago?

His deep, husky voice assured her he was no delusion. "Keeping our date—five weeks later," he told her. "It seems you've been losing your memory. Or did you disappear on me on purpose?"

Dale grabbed her purse and began to slide out of the booth. Burke's hand shot out and captured her wrist, holding it firmly but with little pressure.

"You're not leaving until I've had my say," he growled.

She ignored his words. She didn't take too kindly to men ordering her around. She'd fought her older brother tooth and nail when they were growing up, and then her father when she was eighteen and he decreed she was too young to leave home. She was certainly not intending to give Burke a privilege she'd denied her own male relatives.

"Let go of me," she snapped.

But Burke maintained his hold. "This time you're not escaping," he said firmly. "Maybe you owed me one for disappearing on you the way I did. But now we're even."

Her laugh was brittle. "Even? We'll never be even for the way you hurt—" Damn! She hadn't intended to say that.

"Why don't you go ahead and finish your sentence? The way I hurt you? Do you think I don't realize that? Do you have any idea how I've kicked myself for the way I treated you? And despite your denials and evasions, I know you must have cared for me a great deal to avoid me. You wouldn't be trying to run away from me like a scared rabbit every time I show up if you didn't still care for me."

That stayed her as no physical show of force or order could have done. Dale didn't appreciate being called a coward—even if she had called herself that quite a few times. She put her purse down on the plastic seat and began unbuttoning her coat, fighting the trembling of her hands as she removed the garment.

Burke didn't try to hide his interested glance when he looked at her long-sleeved lime-green shirt and the forest-green wool vest that adhered faithfully to her curves.

"You've lost weight," he said casually as he took her winter jacket and hung it on a nearby coatrack.

"And you haven't lost your eagle eye," she told him crossly. "But reserve it for another woman, please."

"There have been no other women," he told her gravely. At her disbelieving snort, he added, "There can't be anyone else for me, Dale. Not after you."

Her smile was icy. "Really? I was given a different impression."

The waitress approached them to hand Burke a menu, but he waved it away, saying, "I'll just have whatever the lady's having." Dale's breakfast followed quickly, and Burke said, "Why don't you eat? We can talk after you're done. You need some sustenance, and quick, before you waste away."

Dale bit into her eggs, finding that her appetite seemed to have improved tenfold despite the hard knot of anger in her stomach.

"Always so complimentary, Burke," she said acidly. "You'll turn my head."

"I hope so," he said, his eyes roaming over her with naked hunger.

The sexual tension that sprang up between them was almost tangible. But Dale tried to dismiss it. There might always be chemistry between them, but a long-term love was built on more than short-term lust. And their shipboard—or houseboat—romance had been killed the moment he'd abandoned her.

She forced down every bite of her breakfast and felt better able to cope. When Burke's breakfast came, she was tempted to get up and leave, but his mocking glance stopped her. She had survived without him for months; she could survive a few more minutes of his torturing company.

"Okay, let's go to your place and talk," he told her when he was done eating. He got out his wallet, obviously intending to pay for both their breakfasts.

Dale didn't raise a fuss—he could afford it, after all—and while he took care of the bill, she'd disappear. She had proved her point by staying with him while he finished his meal, and she'd already told him several times to leave her alone.

She saw the surprise on Burke's face when he saw her calmly walk out of the restaurant as he stood in line, waiting to pay for their meal. She smiled and waved, then stepped outside into the cold, dismal day.

She walked unhurriedly to her car. As she was pulling away she saw Burke emerge from the restaurant. To make sure he didn't catch up with her, she took a complicated route to the Laundromat. Her marathon sightseeing on first arriving in the city served her well: She knew all the dodges to lose an unwelcome shadow.

Forty-five minutes later, Dale parked in the small mall where the Laundromat was located. Fighting the wind, she got her laundry basket out of the trunk. As she went into the Laundromat, she saw that inside there was only a young couple—obviously still in honeymoon spirit—and an elderly gentleman. She wouldn't have to wait today. After putting her clothes into a machine and feeding the machine the appropriate coins, she sat on one of the stoollike chairs lining the bright yellow and orange room and, taking out a paperback, began to lose herself in a gripping adventure story.

A pair of immaculate black leather shoes came into her line of vision. She didn't know how much time had passed because she'd been so engrossed in the fictional heroine's perils. But she didn't have to look up to know to whom those shoes belonged.

How had he tracked her here?

"There are quite a few Laundromats in this city," he remarked conversationally as he sat in one of the metal chairs next to her. "It took me a while to locate you."

She looked about her and saw that they were now alone in the Laundromat. The couple and the older man had already left. He noticed her apprehensive glance and smiled wolfishly. "Not too many people are venturing out today. There's a storm warning."

"How did you find me at the restaurant? And how did you know I was going to a Laundromat?" she asked, figuring she might as well satisfy her curiosity. She was obviously not going to be able to manage a quick getaway this time. Not with Burke sitting next to her, however deceptively casual his attitude. Not with her clothes still spinning in the washer.

"I got to your apartment just as you were putting the laundry basket in the car. I waited till you drove off, and I followed you." Indicating the deserted Laundromat, he asked, "Aren't you afraid to be here all by yourself?"

She looked at him carefully, trying to determine whether he was trying to scare her. But she pushed the thought away as ridiculous. Burke had promised her once that she had nothing to fear from him. She'd believed him then. She believed it now.

He added smoothly, "Don't worry, I'll protect you."

She sat up and began transferring the load to the dryer.

"I don't need your protection." All she had ever wanted from him was love.

"You mean you're not like all women—wanting a man to protect you and your home and your children?"

She turned from her task and told him, "I'd have thought with your vast experience, you'd know not all women are the same. Or is it that you're only attracted to one type?" She closed the lid savagely and said, "If what I wanted from a man was protection, I'd hire a bodyguard."

He smiled with that white flash of perfect teeth that never failed to affect her bone marrow. She realized how tanned he was and unthinkingly said, "You're even darker than on the *Seaprincess*."

"Like you, I suspect I've put in a lot of long hours. Only I work outside, under the hot sun."

She found that she was curious about him—how he was, where he'd been, what he'd been up to. Yet, she didn't want to ask him anything that would reveal that intense, burning curiosity.

"Burke, why don't you just go? I don't know why you even came back. It's no good..."

He walked slowly toward her and pinned her against the spinning machine. Dale felt the vibrations against her back, but they barely registered in the tumult he was arousing even through his thick coat and her layered clothing.

"I came back because I couldn't get those green eyes out of my mind. Or that luscious body. And above all, the fiery temper and crystal laugh."

"I'm sure you can replace all those, Burke. But I'm not willing to resume a casual relationship—"

"That's not what I want," he interrupted, pressing himself against her. She raised her arms to push him away, but he grabbed them and put them about his waist. "I'm in love with you, Dale."

Those words would have meant a lot on the houseboat. Now they only reminded her of all the times Joel had said the very same thing to hold her to him.

"I'm sure you'll understand if I don't quite believe you," she told him, her voice raw despite her effort to show indifference. "Your note clearly stated that you wanted a clean break and that your job didn't allow for bringing a woman along. So—"

"Will you forget that damn note," he exploded. He pulled away from her a minute, just long enough for him to tear open his parka. "That was a mistake I'll regret all my life. I wasn't sure what it was I felt for you then, but I did know that it was something very deep. So deep that it terrified me, and I ran."

"I'm sorry, but I can't buy that. Your job means and has always meant everything to you. And I won't be second to anything."

"Will you believe this, then," he asked, his voice low and harsh.

His mouth covered hers. This time there was no violence in the kiss. Only untempered hunger and a sense of desperation. The tip of his tongue touched hers gently in greeting. Dale forced herself not to respond, even though her skin felt on fire from his hot, uneven breath and from the touch of his hands, which had burrowed under her blouse and were caressing her back.

"Maybe you think you love me, Burke," she told him when he finally lifted his head, his gaze dark and bleak. "And maybe, in a way, you do. But it would never be enough for me."

He moved away a fraction of an inch to let her breathe more freely. But he maintained close contact with her body, making it hard for her to think coherently

"There's more to this than me, or my note, isn't there?" he challenged her. "You once mentioned that women need survival skills because of men like me. Me and someone else—right?"

She cursed his perfect recall. She didn't feel like going into an explanation about Joel. But she also knew Burke well enough to be sure that he'd demand one.

He tipped her chin with his hand and looked deep into her eyes. "Who was that other man who made you so afraid to trust me?"

She met his glance defiantly. If he wanted the truth, damn him, she'd give it to him! "I wouldn't call it making me afraid. He cured me of looking at life through rose-colored glasses and taught me to look after myself. Joel was a lot like you, Burke. Charming, handsome, witty. He was also an adventurer who liked to have his cake and eat it, too. Oh, I suppose in his way he also loved me. He kept coming back to me, and I don't think he was ever unfaithful to me.

He just wanted to see the world and, when he got home, to have me waiting for him. I lived my life and adapted my schedule to his. We were to be married, and the first time he had good reason to postpone the ceremony. An emergency with work. But the second time, his excuse wasn't that good: He chose not to get married. I guess shackles, as he viewed the bonds of marriage, scared him." She saw understanding dawn on Burke's tanned features and added bitterly, "I was so much in love that I kept making excuses for him, keeping my life in limbo for almost three years, letting my career flounder. The third time we were to be married, I was the one who broke it off. Not because I wanted to get back at him—I still loved him—but because I knew I couldn't live my life on hold. Joel would never change, and I wanted a man who would love me at least as much as he loved his job. I didn't want to be a convenience."

Burke's hand moved from her chin to her cheek, his touch light and loving. He cupped her cheek and said softly, "I'm not Joel, Dale."

"Aren't you?" she asked, smiling bitterly.

"I know I hurt you, but it's not that my job means more to me than you do."

She raised her hand to his, unable to refrain from touching him any longer. Dear Lord, how she loved this man!

"I'm sure you believe what you're saying, Burke. Maybe you could stay with me for a while, but the lure of adventure would take you from me soon. And I refuse to be a camp follower, to live in some spot for days and weeks at a time, awaiting your return. I want a home and family, and as you said, your job is not conducive to family life."

"But I don't expect you to accompany me. As a matter of fact, I'm on the verge of giving up troubleshooting. At least on the scale I've been following till now."

Dale shook her head, absently noting that her clothes had stopped spinning in the machine. "I can't let you give up your job," she told Burke flatly. "It wouldn't be fair for you, since you wouldn't be happy without the excitement and constant travel and danger. And it wouldn't be fair to me, either. I may be selfish, but if I ever marry, I want my husband to myself." Her smile wavered as she added, "And you haven't even talked of marriage, have you?"

His voice was husky when he said, "You haven't given me a chance. I was going to propose—that day after the moving, if you'd been there."

She lifted her hand to his cheek and said softly, "I didn't mean to extract a proposal from you. It's not even so very important to me. Your love is what is most important."

His hand closed over her fingers and pressed them against her cheek. "You have that, Dale. I love you."

She closed her eyes at the husky words, and this time, when his lips touched hers in a butterfly kiss, she responded. But it could never be, she thought. Burke could never be happy with a desk job. He'd fought his father for fifteen years over that issue. And if Burke wasn't at peace with himself, they couldn't be happy together. It was better to end it now, before their relationship had a chance to deepen—and grow more bitter.

"I'm sorry, Burke, but it's no use," she said.

His hand tightened on hers. "But why? If you're still angry about the note—"

"I'm still *hurt,* yes," she corrected softly. "You'll never know how much pain you caused me. I was in love with you even then. That's why I asked you to make love to me."

His eyes closed in silent anguish, and with her finger she traced the long, thick eyelashes, trying to ease his pain.

"But it would never work," she continued in a low voice. "It's better if we end it now."

"A clean break?" he asked, brightness in his blue-green eyes.

She nodded in reply, finding the lump in her throat too large for her to speak.

He smiled bitterly and told her, "Lady, you couldn't have chosen a better method of revenge."

She looked at him, shaking her head. She was not after revenge. Not now. She tried to speak, but Burke anticipated her.

"All the same, I'm not giving up. I know you find it hard to believe me. I have to go away for a week—"

"Of course," she said sadly, remembering all the times Joel had had to go on just this one trip. That one emergency.

His hands went to her shoulders, and he squeezed them as if to imprint belief in her. "I have to go away for a week, but I'll be back. And I plan to have you, sweet lady."

"Dale," she corrected tersely.

"You'll always be my sweet lady, Dale," he told her. "I might have begun calling you that to deny your importance to me, but that's the way I've thought and dreamed of you when I lay in the desert with only the distant stars to keep me company."

He placed a gentle, reverent kiss on her lips and

slid her blouse inside her slacks before stepping back from her.

"Now, let's get your clothes folded. I'll see you home before catching my flight out."

- *11* -

THE PHONE RANG a week later, just as Dale was leaving for work.

"Hayward residence," she said into the receiver.

"Dale? I'm at the airport," Burke said. "I just got in. Wait for me at home."

Dale looked at the receiver in her hand. "Goodbye, Burke," she said into the mouthpiece.

"Dale, don't you dare hang up on me."

She put the phone delicately in its cradle and retraced her steps into the dining room. The bridal shower present she had bought for a friend made a gaudy centerpiece on the table. Picking it up, she gave silent thanks to the invitation to celebrate Cathy McCarthy's upcoming nuptials. It would save her from coming home early tonight.

As soon as she got in to work, her secretary told her that Harvey Nesmond wanted to see her. Dale went up to his office and spent the next hour going over her report on the new resort near Hannibal, as well as a few other ideas she had. Harvey told her about the convention of dentists they'd be having right before Christmas and asked that she supervise it personally.

As she walked down the hall to her office, angry voices reached her—hard, male voices that drowned out softer, feminine ones. Dale hurried toward the pandemonium.

Reaching her office, she saw what the commotion was all about. Burke was there, engaged in an argument with Porthos Lassiter, the head of security.

Porthos, named after Dumas's character in the *The Three Musketeers*, really fit his sobriquet. He was six foot six, a giant of a man, and his massive red head and fierce brown eyes never failed to intimidate. Except today.

Burke was asking for her and not taking no for an answer. As soon as he saw her he began walking toward her, but Porthos put his hammy hand on Burke's shoulder.

"Hold it, buster. You may want to see Ms. Hayward, but it doesn't necessarily follow that she wants to see you."

"Either take your hand off me or wear it in ill health," Burke told him evenly.

Dale got closer to the two men, and Burke looked straight into her eyes. She noticed that his were bloodshot and had deep circles under them. Obviously, he hadn't slept much for a day or two.

"Tell this bozo to get lost, Dale, before someone gets hurt," Burke barked at her.

Porthos's already ruddy complexion turned even

redder. "Ms. Hayward, do you want me to teach this yo-yo some manners?"

His tone was so eager that Dale had to smile. "No, thank you, Porthos. Mr. Sheridan was just leaving."

By now, word of the confrontation had spread, and people from other departments had arrived on the scene, forming a semicircle of spectators around the two men. Dale felt as if she were back in the days of the gladiators.

"You're not afraid for this joker, are you, Dale? I promise I won't harm him—"

"Harm me?" Porthos roared. "I can take you apart with one hand."

"No one is taking anyone apart, gentlemen," Dale said coolly.

Burke agilely sidestepped the security chief. "Dale," he said, "you're going to see me—"

"I think we've said all we have to say."

She met and held his gaze with a calmness she was far from feeling, and saw several emotions warring on Burke's face. Porthos stood next to him, undecided but obviously spoiling for a fight. As she noticed how rigidly Burke was holding himself, Dale wondered idly if he wasn't going to oblige.

But his body visibly relaxed, and he said, "All right, Dale. You win this round. I don't want to jeopardize your job." Throwing off Porthos's hold as if it were a troublesome insect, he added, "But we're not through yet. Expect me this evening."

Everyone began to disperse slowly, and Porthos helped those that were inclined to linger. Dale thanked him and, when he worriedly asked her if she wanted some protection, assured him that Burke was not dangerous—only stubborn.

She went into her office, asking her assistant, Peggy, to hold all calls until lunch. She said a silent prayer of thanks for Burke's willpower—although why she should be grateful was not really clear to her, since he'd started the whole thing. But knowing how both men had wanted to go at each other, she felt that the averted fight was worth any embarrassment she had suffered.

She found it hard to concentrate on her work. Burke's appearance had caused chaos, not only in the office, but also in her own routine. Feeling the need to get away, she went out to lunch that day, although she usually just had a sandwich ordered in from a local deli. Peggy Banks, who had been with the company for five years and had proved to be a very able assistant to Dale, looked at her curiously when she left, but said nothing. Dale said another prayer of silent thanks for Peggy's discretion.

The afternoon passed in a blur of long-distance calls and dictation. Dale stayed on long after Peggy had left, catching up on paperwork until it was time to go to Cathy's bridal shower.

The bridal shower was a happy, crazy affair. Forty women were crowded into a small living room. One of the co-givers of the shower had arranged for a saleslady to give a lingerie demonstration, and that caused endless hilarity as some of the women modeled the sexy, and in some cases almost nonexistent, creations.

While many of the married women had to get back to their families, some of the younger, single women were reluctant to leave. So one of the bridesmaids came up with the idea of seeing the new exotic male dancers at a recently opened club. Dale went along. She found that the show did not particularly impress her, but the cocktails were good and it did help kill the time. However, the attractive, flexible male bodies gyrating on stage made her nostalgic for Burke's exciting, beautiful body.

As she drove slowly home, Dale reran in her mind the marvelous days she'd spent with Burke, and his unexpected persistence of the past few weeks. Could he really be serious about giving up his exciting job to settle down? Or was he only deluding himself? She had felt emotionally battered after the years she'd given to Joel, and what would she go through if she allowed Burke to convince her and he found out that she was not enough of an incentive to keep him in one place? She'd be devastated, she decided.

As she parked the car and walked up to the front door Dale could not even find joy in the first real snow of the season. She trudged through the iridescent mat under her feet, her suede boots moving with a weariness that had nothing to do with the lateness of the hour. Digging automatically into her briefcase for her house keys, she didn't notice the large form in the shadows of the doorway until she was upon it.

"Where the hell have you been?" Burke ground out.

She jumped at the sudden apparition and less-than-welcoming voice. Speechless, she could only stare at the Sasquatch in front of her. Burke was covered with snow from toe to head, his marvelous blond hair a white cap around his head.

"What are you doing here?" she demanded, finally finding her voice. It was almost three o'clock in the morning, and Burke looked as if he'd been standing in the blowing snow for hours.

"Waiting since seven o'clock. I thought I'd give you time to come home, shower, and rest before you and I had our belated talk."

"Burke, I—"

"You're not going to tell me to leave, are you, Dale?"

His tone had grown dangerously icy, matching the weather and his own internal temperature.

It was the latter, not his implied threat, that made her decide to let him in. She knew the only hurt she'd ever endure from Burke was the emotional kind: the desolate hurt she'd felt as her world had tumbled about her, leaving it empty and cold.

"Come in," she told him briskly, opening the front door.

Burke followed her so closely that she was reminded of that other time she'd been trailed by him, when he'd come to her bedroom on the houseboat to give her the coconut oil. This time she could feel only coldness emanating from him.

As Dale stopped in front of her apartment, Burke positioned himself so she couldn't get in unless he allowed it. When she raised a perfectly arched brow at him, he explained pleasantly, "I'd rather not have to break this door in if you decide to try something tricky."

Her green eyes widened innocently, "Why, Burke, how can you think such a thing of me..."

"I learn from experience," he said drolly, his left palm resting on the door frame, his right arm curved about her waist as she opened the door.

He let her precede him, but kept a hold on the door

and then leaned against it once he was inside.

"Burke, you're beginning to make me nervous," she told him as his eyes went over her unreadably. "A woman can never tell about a man. You're giving the impression that you'd like to..."

"Jump on you?" he supplied smoothly. He approached her and looked into green eyes that were trying to appear frightened but were succeeding only in looking mischievous. "That thought has occurred to me, believe me," he went on. "Many things go through a man's head when he's left standing in the cold for"—he looked at his thin gold watch—"eight hours."

"Including murder?" she said, her breathing growing erratic as he came to within an inch of her.

"Right there on top of my list," he said, grabbing the lapels of her winter coat.

Her heart skipped a beat and then whirled away from her. "What others things are there on top of the list?" she asked throatily.

His mouth was hard on hers as he answered, "One, make love to you." Another kiss. "Two, make love to you." Again he kissed her. "And so on until I reach number ten."

"And murder?" she asked, her eyes sparkling, her mouth swollen after ten kisses.

"Right after I take you," he growled, taking her in his arms for a kiss that went on and on until she had no more air left.

She began beating on his shoulders; but he didn't release her right away, apparently unaware of her predicament. It was only when she let herself go slack and he had to hold her up that he finally raised his head and liberated her lips.

"You're terrifying me," she told him when she was at last able to squeeze air into her lungs.

He cupped the back of her head, wreaking havoc with her neat chignon. "I think the cavemen had the right idea when they beat their women and dragged them about by the hair. You're not scared of anything, Dale, including me."

Her features sobered, the tender smile on her kiss-swollen lips fading.

"But I *am* afraid of you, Burke. That's why I've told you to get out of my life. You hurt me so much when you left . . ."

His arms tightened about her. "You know you have nothing to fear from me physically."

"I sensed that from the first," she told him, her eyes soft with remembering. "I have no respect for violent men, men who cannot control their emotions." Her arms rested against his chest as if to maintain closeness while preventing anything further. "And ironically, it was that very strength of character that made me fear an involvement with you. Because I knew how much your work meant to you, and how you'd fought your father, whom you love deeply, to retain freedom and a wanderer's life. And I knew if it came to a choice between your work and me, you'd make the same choice Joel did."

He tilted her head upward and looked at her with fierce eyes. "I've told you before, I'm not Joel."

She pulled at his arms, and reluctantly, he set her free. Moving away from him, she removed her ivory coat and asked him wearily, "Why don't you take off your coat? Warm up a bit before you leave."

He opened his parka with angry fingers, but his voice was even when he said, "I'm not leaving for quite a while. At least, not until I've gotten what I want from you."

Her eyes flew to his and became misty. "If sex is on your mind, you probably won't have too much trouble securing it. My defenses are low this evening."

His eyes flashed, but he didn't move toward her. "I always have sex in mind when I'm around you. That's something that will never change. But I want more from you than sex."

"Why is it that men seem to expect so much, yet want to give so little?" she asked with a small, bitter smile. "I've told you, if you want me to go to bed with you, you can persuade me easily tonight."

"Sort of a farewell gift?"

Her head snapped up. It was true; she wanted to make a gift of herself to Burke. And she was crazy to do it. But she was tired of fighting him, and if he was going to disappear from her life in any case, she could at least have one last memory of him.

"You could call it that," she said. "Why don't you get the fire started in here while I go make you some soup?"

"I'm not hungry. A drink would be welcome, though."

She motioned to the bar in the dining room. "Help yourself. I'm making you some soup."

She went into the kitchen, expecting him to follow. But he didn't. When she went back into the living room with a tray and two steaming mugs of soup, Burke was sitting in front of the fireplace, his tan sweater off, his bronzed back exposed, gleaming seductively as the light danced on the well-defined muscles and created dark hollows in the rib cage and lower back.

He seemed to sense her presence, because he asked, "What's the matter?"

She studied his back silently for a few more seconds, unconsciously comparing his physique with male strippers she'd seen tonight and finding his rivals lacking. The blood rushed to her face and hammered in her veins, and she said flippantly as she placed the tray on the low coffee table and handed him the soup, "Just comparing you to some other men I've seen tonight."

She sat on her rocking chair, out of his line of vision, and Burke didn't turn around at her words.

"Where were you all night?"

"I really don't think I need to account to you for any of my actions, do I? After all, you forfeited any right when you said a clean break would be better."

"You'll never forgive me for that, will you?"

The hatred, which had carried her those horrible first weeks until she'd once more begun to give her life some meaning, was gone. It had been carried away by the frigid winds of autumn. But the hurt remained.

"As we won't be seeing each other again after tonight, it's a moot point, isn't it?" she responded tartly.

His shoulder blades clenched, and his back, so powerful and masculine, suddenly looked very vulnerable. He seemed poised as if to receive a blow.

"Dale, I love you," he said softly.

The quiet words made her shiver. But they were too late. Why couldn't he have said them while they were on the *Seaprincess?*

"I've been through that before, remember?" she answered. "Those words begin to lose their power after a while; when they precede a lengthy absence. I'm sorry, but I'd rather end things now rather than later. This way we can both save ourselves bitterness and accusations."

His mug of soup joined the glass on the floor next to him. Dale's mesmerized eyes followed the clean, strong lines of his back, seeing the stiffness that invaded each muscle.

"So you're not willing to try? To give me a chance?" he asked.

"Burke, I know you," she told him. "You're an adventurer, and adventurers don't thrive staying at home. They have to be out there, building and exploring, looking for new challenges, new danger—"

"Unless they've found an adventure more worthwhile. Unless they've found what they never even knew they were looking for."

Dale's eyes filled with tears as they read the waiting tension in his back. She realized suddenly how vulnerable Burke really was. Anyone opening up to love faced that dangerous possibility: to be devastated by the unexpected, overwhelming emotion. The sense of power that she experienced made her giddy. If she really wanted to hurt him, to get back at him for the pain he'd inflicted, she had no better weapon. Burke was in love with her.

But on the heels of that revelation came another: the fragility of that love, the sense of responsibility that accompanied that power. It had not been love at first sight for either of them, although she'd realized the extent of her feelings sooner than Burke had. He'd been too busy trying to prevent his fall, and what he'd seen as a curtailment of his freedom when he'd discovered after making love to her that she'd gotten under his skin. Then he'd proceeded to try to extricate himself from the danger and to purge Dale from his system.

But that instant infatuation and sexual awareness she'd had of Burke had blossomed into love. She had chosen to take a chance, and had then retreated at the tearing pain that had ensued when Burke had left. And when he had returned, ready to take her on and to make amends, she'd spurned him and kept him at a distance because she didn't want to see history repeated. She'd never wanted to experience that excruciating pain of loss again. In her way, she, too, had been an emotional coward. But Burke had followed his own hard course: from infatuation to frank sexual desire to confronting his own fears. Finally admitting his love for her to himself, he'd begun pursuing her.

Burke had obviously thought she was worth the chance . . . and was now leaving it up to her. Her original feelings about him had been right: He did run deeper than Joel, only it had taken him a while to find himself.

She was about to speak when he got up, his back rigid. "I guess you've given me your answer." He picked up his sweater and slipped it on, then got his coat and walked to the door with a slow, tired stride.

She asked him quietly as he reached the front door, "What about sex? Don't tell me Burke Sheridan is losing his touch?"

He paused with his hand on the doorknob.

"I've told you I wanted more than that. If you can't give me your love, I'd rather leave . . ."

He opened the door and stepped outside. *Out of*

my life, thought Dale. She tried to tell herself it was for the best.

But his palm suddenly hit the open door with a force that made her jump and rock wildly in her chair and caused the door to bounce on its hinges. Some of the soup spilled on her wool suit, and she put the mug on the floor just as Burke slammed the door shut and began walking back into the room.

"Dammit, Dale, I can't leave you."

His wet coat flew across the room and his damp sweater followed. He picked her up as if she weighed no more than a child, and she hung on to his neck in surprise.

"You may hate me in the morning, but I'm going to have to chance it," he told her as he cradled her roughly; he seemed afraid she'd try to escape.

His destination was obviously the bedroom, and his intentions were just as obvious, even though the expression on his face was rather fierce.

"How about the rug in front of the fireplace?" she ventured as she relaxed in his hold and ran her hands over his beautiful back, where the muscles contracted under her touch. She'd been dying to get her hands on that gorgeous male back, and now she sighed as she indulged her skin-hunger.

"I want to inaugurate your bed and leave my mark between your sheets." His words and the images they evoked made her shiver with pleasure.

"I thought you were leaving," she told him as he set her down by her queen-size bed.

"I almost did, until I realized that I couldn't afford to lose you. I'll be thirty-seven next month, and I've always liked kids." He began taking off her jacket.

"Are you expecting to produce a child tonight? If

so, I have some news for you—they take nine months, and besides, I'm protected. So if that's your reason for bedding me . . ."

He was now down to her skirt, her suit jacket and silk blouse lying somewhere on her wine-colored rug. Her side zipper was cooperating marvelously with his impatient fingers.

His ordinarily impassive countenance was full of purpose and passion. "My reason for taking you to-night is to drive you crazy until you admit you love and will marry me. I was a fool to walk out on you once, but then, that is par for the course. I've been an idiot since I met you—probably my brain cells began to burn up—but if I made a stupid mistake in leaving you and writing that note I intend to make up for it the rest of our lives."

She stood passively in his arms until he'd gotten rid of her slip and hose and left her in only her bra and panties. When he began unbuckling his belt, his eyes on hers, she said to him, "I told you that you might convince me to make love to you tonight—or, the way things are going, to have you make love to me tonight. But marriage requires more extensive, intensive cooperation. I've always pictured a part-nership, and I don't think that's what you have in mind right now."

His pants, accompanied by his briefs, flew down his legs as if they had wings. Dale recalled how Burke had positively no inhibitions, and she appreciated his sensitivity in letting her keep on a minimum of cloth-ing, even in his passionate rage. Even though she knew she wouldn't keep them on for long.

Her eyes looked down his body with interest, and he hardened visibly under her gaze. Her lips curved into a satisfied smile, and he went suddenly alert, stomping on his high-running emotions to say suspiciously, "You don't seem to be putting up much of a fight."

"You've been too busy with your dominant, macho performance to realize it, have you?" she replied.

He picked her up and swung her high in the air. She didn't even squeal, secure in the knowledge he'd be there to catch her. Now that he'd committed himself, she was sure he'd be there for her from this moment on. And she trusted him enough to let the questions wait until later.

"Don't scare easy, do you," he said, putting a knee on the bed and depositing her gently on it.

"Should a woman have something to fear from the man she loves?" she asked him softly as he disposed of her bra and panties.

He let his weight fall on her roughly and she welcomed it, just as she welcomed his swift, hungry parting of her legs. Tonight there would be no preliminaries—at least, not the first time.

"You mean you were going to let me walk out that door?" he asked incredulously. "Even though you profess to love me?"

"Why not? You've certainly had enough practice," she answered him as she buried her fingers in the silky springiness of his hair.

"Really?" His hand sought some silky hair also, but farther down her body. He pressed against the soft mound.

Her breath caught in her throat as his fingers prepared her for his entrance. "Yes. Now retaliate for my cynicism with instant and constant ravishment. You'll get my full cooperation, of course."

He opened her legs wider and thrust inside. "I don't think it can be termed ravishment if you cooperate. But I'll certainly give your idea some thought."

She gasped at his hot invasion. "Please do," she murmured, arching her hips to receive him deeper and smiling at the groan that erupted from his throat. She placed a kiss at the base of his neck. "Oh, Burke," she whispered, "don't stop what you're doing."

"No chance, lady," he told her throatily before his mouth fused with hers.

- *12* -

"I'D LIKE TO know why you had me ask my boss for a week off," Dale said as Burke spirited her away in her car the following morning.

They had spent the previous day in bed, with only occasional forays into the kitchen and the shower, and Burke had rushed her out of her apartment a short while ago after instructing her to pack an overnight case.

"Tomorrow's Thanksgiving. You might as well co-ordinate a mini-vacation with a national holiday."

"Thanksgiving." Her brain was beginning to function again, now that Burke's hands and lips were temporarily idle. "You're taking me to your parents' house," she guessed, recognizing the way to the airport.

He nodded. "I'd like you to meet my parents and the rest of the clan." Picking up her hand, he stroked her palm and said, "I have some news for my father."

Her head shot up and Burke's eyes met hers. She knew what he meant, and her heart tripped over itself in sudden confusion and excitement.

She also realized that Burke was allowing her some room, some time to think things over. She'd been adamant about believing that he was the same as Joel. He was now trying to prove her judgment wrong. He was asking for a chance.

Her fingers closed about his, but she didn't answer. Yesterday, Burke had convinced her that he was in love with her. What remained was for her to be convinced he had staying power.

And Dale knew that only she could make that ultimate decision. She'd given Burke her love... now he awaited her trust...

When they arrived in Elizabeth, New Jersey, they encountered a winter wonderland. The snowfall had been heavy and children played on the sidewalks and in the parks, running their sleds and diving into high hills of snow as if into a pool.

Dale studied the house as she got out of the taxi, seeing it pretty much as she'd pictured it; a big, white, rambling house with a huge backyard where children had played and dreamed and grown.

Apparently, they were expected, because an older couple opened the door and stepped eagerly outside. Both of them were in their sixties, tall and handsome, with their blond hair gracefully turning silver.

"Come in, come in," the woman Dale knew must be Jeannine Sheridan said, opening the door and bustling them through. She hugged Burke while Wayne Sheridan slapped him heartily on the back, love-strong thumps that would have felled a lesser man. Burke hugged his mother and then embraced his father, shaking his hand. Dale noticed that Wayne Sheridan had blue eyes, while Jeannine's were a deep, lovely green.

After the warm, effusive welcome, Burke laced his arm about Dale's waist and told his parents, "Mom, Dad, this is Dale Hayward. I think I may have mentioned her once or twice."

"Once or twice!" Wayne exclaimed while Jeannine hugged her. He gave Dale a hearty hug in turn and, stepping back, added, "My son certainly has good taste."

"What my husband means is that Burke has never brought a woman friend of his to meet us before," Jeannine put in quietly. "And we're very happy to have the chance to get to know you."

His eyes running appreciatively over Dale's figure-hugging hunter-green coat, Wayne Sheridan said, "Not only intelligent but beautiful."

"But you don't know me yet," Dale protested, warmed but overwhelmed by such an enthusiastic reception.

"Any woman who would make my son squirm after the stunt he pulled deserves a medal," Wayne replied.

"You mean you know?" Dale asked, her cheeks warming at the implications of that statement.

"About his leaving you on the *Seaprincess* and your not wanting to have anything to do with him for months?" Wayne said, clapping Burke on the back. "Yep. He came here before going to St. Louis the first time to set things right. He told us he had found a very special woman but through his own fault had about lost her, and we've been anxiously awaiting the outcome these past few weeks."

Jeannine Sheridan noticed Dale's discomfort and

said, "Come into the living room. It's chilly in the hallway, and we have a lovely blaze going." She put her arm around Dale's waist and led her inside. "Here, give me your coat and make yourself at home."

Jeannine gave the garment to Wayne to hang up and patted the couch as she sat down. "Sit here with me, dear." Dale sat, somewhat uneasy at being an open book to these charming, affectionate people. She could see where Burke came by his uninhibited nature. "Now, don't worry about the revelations Burke made," Jeannine said comfortably. "He certainly didn't disclose any intimate details, if that's what's troubling you."

"That's, ah—reassuring," Dale murmured, her eyes seeking Burke's. He was leaning on the mantel in front of the fireplace, and she threw him visual daggers.

Wayne came back into the room and sat on the other side of her. Dale felt suffocated.

"What did I miss?"

"Mother was just telling Dale how open we are with each other and how we never keep secrets," Burke said, his eyes glinting with wicked amusement.

"Now, that's not true, Burke, and you know it," Jeannine chided him and patted Dale's hand. "Pay no attention to him, dear. He's a born troublemaker. Takes after his father."

"Now, Jeannine, don't go spreading nasty, false tales about me," Wayne said. His wife answered him in kind, sparking a lively debate. It was obvious how much they loved each other.

Dale began recovering her equilibrium. She hadn't realized how intimidating meeting one's prospective in-laws could be; it had taken the stuffing out of her for a few minutes. But as she realized how sincere and warm they were, and how very welcome she was in this family, she began to relax. But Burke would certainly pay for having fun at her expense. As her gaze met his once more it promised him heavy retribution.

The next couple of hours passed swiftly. The maid came and went, and the cook was given the evening and the following day off. Dale learned that Jeannine and Wayne would be in charge of the Thanksgiving feast and that some of the dishes, like salads and pastries, had already been prepared.

She found herself recounting her life story, telling the Sheridans very revealing things. Dale recognized wryly what a smart, wily woman Jeannine was—no doubt she made an excellent, feared lawyer. She and Wayne were perfectly matched. Dale was happy to discover what a wonderful role model of a marriage Burke had grown up with.

She noticed his intense interest when certain aspects of her life were revealed, although he didn't say much. He preferred to listen and absorb as Dale was charmingly grilled, going from her toddler years all the way through college and her current job. And, Dale admitted to herself, she was hopelessly captivated by Burke's vivacious parents in the process.

Refreshments were regularly offered and pressed upon her—probably to ensure that she lived through her ordeal, Dale thought—until she was convinced she'd float away. When she refused cold cuts, hors d'oeuvres, and dinner, as well as another drink, tea, coffee, and hot chocolate, Burke intervened.

"I think Dale would like to rest." His quiet words stopped the lively interrogation, and both Sheridans apologized instantly.

"Of course, how thoughtless of us..."Jeannine apologized.

"Sorry, Dale," Wayne Sheridan said gruffly. "It's such a pleasure to see this arrogant, footloose son of mine brought down that I got carried away."

Burke didn't much care for his father's words, but Dale smiled warmly at Wayne and hugged his arm as the Sheridans walked her to the stairway.

"I'll go up with you, dear," Jeannine decided. "I wasn't sure if you and Burke wanted one or two rooms..." she began tactfully.

"Separate rooms will be fine," Dale said quickly before Burke could speak.

Displeasure was evident in his rugged features.

Jeannine smiled charmingly and said, "Burke, get Dale's suitcase, will you?"

"I'm afraid I only have an overnight case," Dale said dryly, doubting that her sharp-eyed possible mother-in-law had not noticed that fact. "Burke was in a great hurry today and didn't give me a chance to take much with me." She didn't add that he hadn't even told her where they were going at first, or that the reason they'd rushed out of the house was that they'd spent the morning making love.

Jeannine hooked her arm through Dale's as they went up the stairs. "Burke has always been the hyperactive one in the family. His younger brothers are more normal, thank heavens."

"I heard that, Mom," Burke said, bringing up the rear, carrying Dale's case and purse.

"That's good, darling. We wouldn't want you to

get a swelled head just because you were lucky enough to snag Dale, would we?"

Apparently, it was a foregone conclusion that Dale would be marrying Burke. She tried to hide her nervousness, as well as keep a level head. The prospect of marrying Burke seemed more and more attractive by the minute.

Wayne Sheridan called from the bottom of the stairs, "But what about dinner, Dale? You look like you need some feeding."

Dale's gaze met Burke's as she looked down and he winked. She had to stop herself from chuckling at Wayne's echoing of his son's concern.

"I think I'll skip it. I'm rather tired and I'd prefer some rest. See you tomorrow," Dale told Burke's father.

"Good night, Dale. It was a real pleasure meeting you," he called up to her.

"Likewise," she replied warmly.

Jeannine showed Dale to her room, which was at one end of the hallway. "Burke's room will be over there," she said, indicating the other end of the corridor.

Burke scowled and Jeannine patted his cheek. "Now, don't be impatient, Burke. You have to allow Dale some rest."

Dale turned a vivid pink, and Jeannine poked her head into the room to make sure everything was in order. Giving Dale a hug and kissing her on the cheek, she said, "Do call us if you need anything. Good night."

"Goo—good night," Dale managed, overwhelmed by her recent ordeal and Jeannine's advice to Burke.

Dropping the case and purse unceremoniously onto

the floor, Burke locked the door behind him and snared her arms, pulling her against him.

"What kind of a stunt is that, asking for separate rooms?" he demanded.

"What kind of a stunt is feeding me to the sharks? Your parents are lovely people Burke, but I felt like that tortured saint who asked that they turn him over when he was done on one side of the grill."

His hands rubbed over the tired muscles of her back and worked their way over to her inner thighs, which were sore from so much nocturnal exercise and unaccustomed stretching.

"You'll miss my wonderful massages," he tempted,, his lips beginning a fiery trail on her neck.

Dale sighed and said, "I'll live. And besides, I really do need to recuperate. I don't think there's an untouched, intact muscle in my body. You drove me insensate after your continuous ravishment."

"Which reminds me, I haven't ravished you lately." He picked her up and carried her to the single bed.

"So you haven't," she told him, letting her hand trail past his stomach and resting it against his zipper.

He bounced her on the bed and threw himself on top of her. The springs squeaked ominously. "You're just asking for it."

"Show me no mercy," Dale whispered as she ran her hands up and down his back and then laced them about his neck.

His eyes told her that mercy was the last thing on his mind as his head obscured the overhead light. But just as his lips met hers, a knock sounded on the door.

"Burke, are you in there? I need you to run an errand for me. We forgot to get pudding mix, and you know that's the only dessert Scott will eat."

Burke sighed in exasperation and buried his face in the front of Dale's winter-white dress.

"Mom, Scott can make do without pudding for one meal."

"Burke, dear, when you have children, you'll want us to have everything they prefer handy—"

"I'll get it later, Mom."

"The stores are about ready to close, dear. And your father is already running another errand for me."

"My mother, the iron general," Burke muttered against the soft twin pillows.

"I heard that, dear. Now, you don't want to give Dale a bad impression of the family, do you?"

Burke sat up disgruntedly and ran his hand through his hair. "I'd better go," he told Dale apologetically. "I may be almost thirty-seven, and I face dangers constantly, but around here I'm only 'Burke, dear.'"

Dale ran her hand from his knee to his thigh and back down. "It helps to keep you humble," she quipped.

His hand automatically stilled hers, and he said, "Dale..."

But the look in her eyes must have stopped him. Or perhaps the inappropriateness of the moment, when they could be interrupted again.

Dale only knew she was grateful for the reprieve. There were too many things to think over, too many feelings and observations to assimilate. She welcomed the breathing space and the promise of a solitary night.

He dropped a swift kiss on her lips, and whispered, "I'll try to sneak in later. Leave the door open for me."

Dale smiled but didn't answer. Burke frowned at her lack of response, and her grin widened as she thought that Burke really was used to having his own way. No wonder his mother had taken him on to give her some respite.

Burke walked to the door with angry strides. He paused before he opened it and told her belligerently, "Until later."

Dale smiled and blew him a kiss.

The door closed with barely leashed violence.

- *13* -

DALE CHECKED HER appearance in the dresser mirror before venturing outside the room. It was almost ten, and the sound of children squealing and screaming had awakened her from a deep, restorative sleep. She'd heard Burke last night. He'd knocked discreetly on her door after midnight—but she hadn't responded to his overture. She'd thought her silence would serve him right for his teasing. But above all, she'd wanted to have some time to herself after their intense interlude.

She'd slept dreamlessly, and her cheeks had the pink of health once more. She'd blow-dried her hair after a long, leisurely bath, and had braided it into a thick coronet.

Now, if she only had the proper clothes for a family gathering. Besides the dress she'd worn yesterday, she'd brought only a pair of pants and a sweater.

Which were what she had on now.

She smoothed the maroon sweater over her hips

once more and rearranged the cuffs of her gray slacks about her suede boots. Running her hand over her thick raven coronet, she left the room.

Famished, she quickened her steps at the delicious smells that assaulted her when she reached the landing. But as she put her foot on the first step, her high, thin heel slipped on something and she found herself jumping several steps at once, then taking the rest of them on her derriere.

The object her heel had encountered landed on the bottom step an instant before she did. Many pairs of eyes turned to watch as the commotion that preceded her sudden appearance cut into the lively conversation.

An adorable curly-haired child who had been by the steps when her forced landing occurred pointed at her and said, "Fall. Girl. Stupid."

His tactless words galvanized the adults into action. Burke reached her first and examined her for broken bones.

"This could get to be a habit," he told her aloud. As the others appeared, he whispered, "That'll teach you to try to drive me insane."

A striking redhead slapped Burke's hands away and examined Dale herself. "Stay away, you lecherous man," she rebuked him. "Let the poor girl alone."

"This is Alice Sheridan," Burke said dryly. "Nurse par excellence, but as a sister-in-law she leaves much to be desired."

A tall, blond-haired man put his arms about Alice's waist and told Burke, "Watch it, big brother. That's my wife you're criticizing."

As Dale got up slowly—or rather, was lifted by Burke under the arms—Burke said, "This is my younger brother, Lee. Resident bookworm.''

"My, you have a sour temperament. I wonder what's making you go around like a bear with a sore head this morning.''

Another blond young man stepped forward and put out his hand. "Before my brother damns *me* with faint praise, allow me to present myself. I'm Darryll Sheridan.''

As Dale shook hands with Burke's youngest brother, another little boy looked up at her and, apparently satisfied that she wasn't dangerous, grabbed on to her pants with sticky caramel fingers, transferring the remnants of a candied apple to the wool.

"Wayne!" Alice scolded, apologizing profusely and attempting to clean up the sticky spot.

Dale leaned against Burke for support and said, "Really, it's all right. Don't worry about it . . .''

"My, my. What happened here?" Jeannine asked, approaching at as fast a pace as she could while carrying the third member of the triplets. "Emily came and got me. She told me there'd been an awful accident.''

"Acci—acc-dent . . .'' Emily echoed from the comfort of her grandmother's arms, her big blue eyes peeping curiously at the stranger. Her hand, full of flour, unerringly aimed at Dale's slightly disheveled hair.

But her father was there to stop the chubby finger from connecting with its intended target.

Emily's face screwed up into an angry frown. "Hair. Pretty hair. Want black hair.''

Dale smiled weakly, and Lee said, "Don't worry. We won't let these monsters scalp you.''

Everyone laughed, and Wayne Sheridan blew into

the house along with a frigid wind. Walking over to the family congregated about Dale, he asked, "What's going on here?"

"Dale fell down the stairs," Alice told him. Seeing the worried look that crossed Wayne's features, she hurried to explain, "Don't worry, Dad. Dale's okay." She looked for the one-third of the triplets not readily visible, and added, "But one young man is not going to be okay. The one whose truck Dale slipped on."

When the young imp in question didn't appear, Alice raised her voice commandingly. "Scott. Where are you? Show yourself."

Scott's angelic face peeped from behind Darryll's jeans, and Alice said, "Come here, young man."

The brown eyes widened in alarm a moment before the blond head disappeared once more behind Darryll's legs.

Dale held on to Burke's waist and said, "It's okay, Alice. No permanent damage done. I'll just sit on pillows for a couple of days."

"Darryll Sheridan, will you stop hiding that child," Alice scolded, not easily mollified. Dale could understand where she'd want to have the upper hand. Already she spied Scott's brother, Wayne, heading for the coffee table where a dish of mints graced the walnut surface. Predictably, the crystal dish tipped over, and Alice turned to face the new catastrophe.

"Wayne Sheridan," she said sternly.

"I'll take that one. You take this one," Lee said calmly, handing Emily to Darryll.

As Alice bent to retrieve Scott from his hiding place Burke said evenly, "Now that you've all met Dale, I'm going to spirit her away for a little while. We'll just take a turn about the property."

Dale's eyes looked longingly at the breakfast she glimpsed being kept warm on a side table in the dining room, and felt her thoughts echoed in Wayne's words.

"Burke, let the poor woman eat. This is no time to go walking, especially not in that blizzard outside. And definitely not on an empty stomach."

Dale began limping toward the dining room, blessing Wayne Sheridan's understanding nature. Apparently, she and Burke's father did have a lot in common, particularly their healthy respect for food.

But her progress was impeded by Burke's arm around her waist, which closed about her with talonlike strength.

"Later, Dad," Burke intervened. "Dale has something she needs to discuss with me, and this way she'll be able to better appreciate and partake of the wonderful Thanksgiving dinner you and Mom are preparing."

Burke led her away, and Dale was only able to sneak another hungry glimpse of the delicious-smelling breakfast before he had her bundled up in coat, cap, and scarf.

Pushing the cap away from her nose, where it tended to settle—Dale thought it very fitting that Burke's head should be so much larger than hers—she asked him frostily, "What's the idea of this cruel and unusual punishment? Is taking me out on an empty stomach in this winter storm, when we can't even see two inches in front of us, your idea of a leisurely stroll?"

Burke pulled her closer into his body, his knowledge of his parents' house and grounds apparently enough to guide him about. He certainly couldn't see much in the white blanket that enveloped them.

"And here I thought that you loved me enough to suffer any deprivation for me," he replied teasingly.

"Not unless it's absolutely necessary," Dale said. "And especially not on Thanksgiving Day. Didn't you ever hear that this one holiday, of all others, is meant to give thanks and to appreciate food? I'll be quite inclined to do the first if I can get some of the latter."

"It's good to find out little things about you, like the fact that I'll have to feed you if I expect to get your undivided attention," Burke said playfully. "Obviously, hunger makes you less sociable."

"So you've discovered my terrible guilty secret," Dale retorted. "Let's go back now."

As she tried to retrace her steps, he picked her up and carried her a few feet, sitting down with her in his lap.

"You certainly seem to have developed a penchant for lifting me up," she told him as she looked about her. Everything was blurry, and she couldn't even see the house any longer. "I thought you once told me I was heavy."

"This is the best way for me to get my daily exercise," he told her, shifting her to get something out of his pocket. "Much more fun than lifting weights."

She leaned over his knees to scoop up some snow and rubbed his mouth with it. "In case that was an insult, I'm washing your mouth out."

He pressed his cold lips upon hers. "Nothing like taking precautionary measures."

One arm left her waist as he grabbed her hand and placed a velvet box in it.

"Open it," he said hoarsely.

As Dale followed his direction, she shielded the contents of the box with one hand.

Inside gleamed a diamond-and-emerald ring.

"It was the closest I could come to the color of your eyes," Burke told her.

When Dale didn't say anything, he shifted on the swing.

"Dale, I want to marry you. I know I hurt you when I left the *Seaprincess* that way, but I—"

She put her cold hand on his mouth and looked up with tears and snowflakes gracing her dark lashes.

"I know. And I accept. I love you, Burke."

His mouth came down on hers with desperate force, and Dale held the opened box tightly in her hand. She'd had plenty of time last night to think things through, and although she had still been scared up until his actual proposal, the words had come naturally from her. She loved Burke, and had loved him for what seemed like forever. He'd broken her defenses in St. Louis, and whatever reservations she'd continued to have had been melted by the warmth of Burke's love and the warmth of his family. Seeing him interact with the Sheridan clan had shown her another facet of Burke, which she'd found just as irresistible as the rest of him.

He slid the ring onto her finger. It was a bit loose.

"I'll either have to make that smaller or else fatten you up a little," he teased. "Dad's worried sick about you."

"We'll worry about that later," Dale murmured, turning around in his lap and closing her thighs about his waist.

The swing rocked wildly, but Burke braced his legs and grabbed her thighs, holding them about him as his lips met hers once more.

"I'll be telling Dad he's finally won the war," he

told her, long, delicious minutes later.

She hugged him, feeling warm and cozy despite the temperature and the snow blowing all about them.

"I'm glad—your dad will be happy. I really like him, you know."

"And he adores you. Just as I predicted." He cupped her chin and lifted it, bending his head to look into her eyes. "I was also thinking about changing the firm's name to Brown, Sheridan, and Sheridan. Do you think you'll mind commuting from New Jersey to St. Louis if I open a branch in the Midwest?"

"I'll definitely give that some thought," Dale told him, slowly raising her arm until her fingers were splayed in his hair. Then she ruffled the crisp tendrils, sending a heavy shower of snow down his neck and face.

Burke got up, her legs about his waist, and dropped his arms. Dale hung on to his neck for dear life.

"Convince me not to drop you," he told her huskily.

She pressed her lips to his, and his arms climbed about her once more.

"You're sure easy to convince," she murmured as he began walking toward the house.

"Can't say the same about you," he told her, his teeth nibbling on her exposed ear. Her cap had been lost somewhere along the way.

"Which reminds me," he told her as she slid her legs from about his waist and began to walk beside him. "Whatever happened to the model of the *Seaprincess?*"

"It's sitting safe and sound in my closet," she assured him.

"I was afraid you'd broken it in anger," he ventured.

Hearing the vulnerability in his voice, she hugged his waist tightly. "I was tempted, but I just couldn't destroy our love. Not even symbolically."

He stopped as they got to the house, kissing her and tasting her once more. Dale breathed in the wonderful scent of him, which was combined with the fresh fragrance of snow, and buried her fingers in his damp, silky hair.

"We must put that replica in a place of honor," he declared. "After all, it was the houseboat that originally brought us together."

As they walked up the steps, she answered, "How about taking a honeymoon on the original—weather permitting? I still have three days—and nights—coming to me."

Burke paused before going into the house and giving his father the news he'd been waiting for so long.

"You'll have more than three days and nights coming to you." He clasped his arms about her waist and nuzzled her throat and cheek. Against the skin that was warmed quickly by his heat and touch, he whispered, "My wandering days are over. You'll have forever."

WONDERFUL ROMANCE NEWS!

Do you know about the exciting SECOND CHANCE AT LOVE/TO HAVE AND TO HOLD newsletter? Are you on our *free* mailing list? If reading all about your favorite authors, getting sneak previews of their latest releases, and being filled in on all the latest happenings and events in the romance world sounds good to you, then you'll love our SECOND CHANCE AT LOVE and TO HAVE AND TO HOLD Romance News.

If you'd like to be added to our mailing list, just fill out the coupon below and send it in...and we'll send you your *free* newsletter every three months — hot off the press.

☐ *Yes, I would like to receive your free SECOND CHANCE AT LOVE/TO HAVE AND TO HOLD newsletter.*

Name _____

Address _____

City _____ **State/Zip** _____

Please return this coupon to:

Berkley Publishing
200 Madison Avenue, New York, New York 10016
Att: Rebecca Kaufman

74

Second Chance at Love.®